Light and Power

*First selection of the second annual
Associated Writing Programs'
Award Series for Short Fiction*

Light and Power.
Stories by Ian MacMillan

University of Missouri Press
Columbia & London, 1980

For Susan, with this
from the beginning

The author wishes to express his appreciation to the editors and publishers of the journals in which these stories first appeared for permission to reprint: "The Rock" in *Hawaii Review* 2:2 (Spring/Fall 1974), reprinted by permission of the University of Hawaii Board of Publications; "The Rat's Eye" in *TriQuarterly* 40 (Fall 1977); "Light and Power" in *The Georgia Review* 22:1 (Spring 1968); "Ashes" is reprinted from *The Massachusetts Review* 10:3 (Fall 1969), copyright© 1969 The Massachusetts Review, Inc.; "Idiot's Rebellion" in *Little Magazine* 12:1–2 (1979); "The Gravity of the Situation" in *Ball State University Forum* 14:2 *(Spring 1973), copyright©* 1973 *Ball State University Forum;* "Corrigan's Progress" in *The Falcon* 5 (Winter 1972); "Sacrifice," *TriQuarterly* 36 (Spring 1976); "The Drive" in *Ball State University Forum* 20:1 (Winter 1979), copyright© 1979 *Ball State University Forum.*

University of Missouri Press, Columbia, Missouri 65211
Library of Congress Catalog Card Number 79-3066
Printed and bound in the United States of America

Library of Congress Cataloging in Publication Data

MacMillan, Ian T
    Light and power.

    CONTENTS: The rock.—The rat's eye.—Light and power.—Ashes.—Idiot's rebellion.—The gravity of the situation. [etc.]
    I. Title.
PZ4.M16673Li   [PS3563.A318955]   813'.5'4   79-3066
ISBN 0-8262-0289-6

Foreword

Reading the stories of Ian MacMillan, you soon get the feeling that you're in good hands. He is both sensitive and responsible—a rarer combination than it may seem.

There is a richness of texture in his work, and a sure sense of pace. Subtleties don't escape his attention, but he knows better than to dwell on them at the reader's expense. His stories keep moving and turning until they end on just the note of satisfying complexity he has had in mind for them all along.

Light and Power was chosen from among twenty short-story collections, each of them culled from a total of 138 book manuscripts submitted in the second annual Associated Writing Programs short-story contest. It was a close decision. There were many good stories by other writers, even a few remarkable ones that anybody would have hated to pass over, but too often those achievements were flanked by material that seemed to have been written in order to justify a table of contents. It was the consistency of MacMillan's performance that made his book stand out.

As a rule I'm not much interested in tales of hazardous snorkeling because they tend to be solemnly told, but MacMillan saves his story "The Rock" with a healthy injection of irony. The hero is a dilettante at danger, and knows it. So does his wife, and so will you—which doesn't keep the underwater stuff from being vivid and scary.

Some readers may quail on learning that the narrator of "The Rat's Eye" is a carnival geek whose crowd-pleasing specialty is gnawing the heads off live rats, but there's no cause for alarm: it turns out to be an oddly graceful, well-written story.

There's a nice mixture of humor and distress in the desperate events of the title piece, "Light and Power." And that happens again, differently, in "Corrigan's Progress": a young rural misfit, never able to do anything right, manages to wound himself in a hunting accident and must then fight for survival while obsessed with envy of people who never make mistakes—especially of the cool, maddeningly competent astronauts then settling on the moon.

In "Sacrifice," when a lifeguard gives mouth-to-mouth resuscitation to a dying girl on a deserted beach, the author takes an admirable risk in allowing strong sexual overtones to pervade the incident. And the risk pays off: this is one of the best stories in the book.

But I think my personal favorite is "The Drive," in which a farm boy and his grandfather struggle to herd cows through a deadly blizzard. The action alone is enough to keep you engrossed in this one; there are plenty of larger implications, arising naturally and conveyed with skill, but it's only fair to let you discover them for yourself.

I want to wish Mr. MacMillan a long and full career. It's a difficult profession, but nobody has to tell him that: if he didn't know it, he couldn't have written so well.

Richard Yates
June, 1979

Contents

AWP Selection in Short Fiction

The selection of Ian MacMillan's *Light and Power* by final judge Richard Yates marks the completion of the second year of the Associated Writing Programs' *AWP Award Series for Short Fiction*, and the second year of the winning manuscript's publication by the University of Missouri Press. Last year's winner, selected by Wallace Stegner, Rebecca Kavaler's *Further Adventures of Brunhild*, has received outstanding critical response. Further, two authors whose work received recognition as finalists in last year's program, Alvin Greenberg and Gladys Swan, have received publishing contracts for their short fiction collections through AWP's program.

Light and Power comes highly recommended, not only by Richard Yates, but by the AWP panel of readers in this year's program, which included: Henry Bromell, Jack Cady, Robert Canzoneri, Pat Carr, Raymond Carver, H.E. Francis, Paul Friedman, Lester Goldberg, David Huddle, Josephine Jacobson, Rebecca Kavaler, Ursule Molinaro, Guy Owen, William Peden, John Stewart, Barry Targan, and Allen Wier. Each manuscript submitted was read by at least two of these distinguished fiction writers.

Richard Yates lives and writes in Boston. He is the author of *Revolutionary Road, Eleven Kinds of Loneliness, A Special Providence, Disturbing the Peace, The Easter Parade*, and the recently highly acclaimed novel, *A Good School*.

Gordon Weaver, managing editor of the *AWP Award Series for Short Fiction* since its inception, is Professor of English and chairman of the department at Oklahoma State University. The author of three novels and three collections of stories, the most recent of which are *Getting Serious* and *Circling Byzantium*, he has received the St. Lawrence Award for Fiction and the 1979 first prize in the annual O. Henry Awards for his work.

The Rock

Calder hits the water with the gleeful vigor of a boy, resisting the shocking cold by churning his legs in a burst of muscular energy. He aims himself at the mysterious, giant rock rising out of the deep water at the mouth of the bay. It is over a mile from shore and halfway there are the crushing breakers which will curl on him with unpredictable ferocity. He has been told more than once that sharks infest the area of the rock, and he has been toying with the idea of cautious approach now for six or seven trips out. Today he has decided that he will make it all the way. He has only been diving four months, but his equipment—fins, mask, snorkel, and spear—all show the satisfying scratches and salt stains of frequent use. He churns along using more force than he needs to because he likes to resist the gentle and powerful motions of the water, likes to challenge its vast, soft bulk.

There is something else—it is the quick and surrealistic, silent pastel brutality of the ocean. Perpetually amazed by it, he regards himself as a humble alien in the last real wilderness, moving in clumsy slow motion in an environment where survival depends on absolute attention. He has been eyeing the rock for months, has been venturing out farther and farther, through the violent and turbulent waves and into the relative calm of the twenty feet of water outside of the reef. He has gone as far as two-thirds of the way without encountering anything odd except very large and dangerous looking moray eels and some different fish. He is drawn to the rock, trudges along using more energy than he needs to use, enjoying the mummified fear somewhere at the back of his mind thinking, stripped almost naked for it. Stripped down to nothing but a goddamned pathetic bathing suit almost a mile offshore in a place whose only sound is the hum and the ticking of a buzzing confusion of life and me, the humble alien, who trades in gravity for its opposite, goggle-eyed and frightened and enjoying every second.

Calder is a New Yorker in Hawaii. He got his year here through a few tricky manipulations of influence, losing a casual friend or two and probably gaining back two or three who would turn out to be more valuable than the ones lost. He designs air-conditioning systems, and he was here only three weeks before he settled into his normal, lazy routine, a continuation of what he did in New York, almost nothing in the morning, drink a little too much at lunch, occupy a house a small notch above his means. Until he discovered the water, there was little that interested him here after the initial one week introduction to what he decided was a corrupted paradise. Not considering the water, here he lived in the moist laziness of a perpetual New York summer without the familiar urban discomforts. Half the secretaries were oriental, half the men you dealt with were oriental, you could not get the New York Times when it was fresh enough to read. In the evening you drank either your own or someone else's Scotch, or you entertained at your house or were entertained at someone else's.

The rilled sand passes under him slowly and he feels like a slow motion bird, his eyes darting into the corners of his limited field of vision and his legs churning along with more energy than he needs to move at a good pace. He raises his head out into the noisy wind and eyes the enlarging rock. Feels the fear and the eerie hollowness of the unexpected lying out there, jaws open, just beyond the pastel limit of his vision. Thinking, nobody near, so vulnerable, out of yell's reach, close to obliteration without a trace.

Calder is thirty-two and not usually inclined to introspection, but the water and its ticking silence and its pastel madness of life and his own freakish isolation almost a mile out turn his mind into itself with him thinking nearly without words, naked and alone with fear and tense-jawed excitement you really feel *here*, don't you, really, breathing hard enough to hurt your lungs. He slows down, gasping through the snorkel, through the little death rattle of collected water at the bottom of the U, thinking, I can really breathe—Jesus, I can really . . .

When he discovered the water he stopped smoking. He had smoked all his adult life and quit with the convert's zeal. One could not pay him a hundred dollars to smoke. Once after four days he bought a pack and tried one cigarette, crushed the rest of the pack and cast it into a sewer. He felt ten pounds lighter. His face broke out with pimples as if he were fifteen again and sexual desire bloomed in a sort of innocent lust. His wife accepted the benefits of this change with good-natured amazement. The feeling drove him out of his office on warm afternoons and up to the university cafeteria to sit by the window and watch the braless girls ride by all perky-assed and jiggly and lean on their ten-speed bicycles. Just to watch, because they all seemed so beautiful. He had never realized how beautiful they really were.

Stranger yet than chemical innocence and lust was memory. It was reborn. He could remember with glassy clarity things he had forgotten by the time he was sixteen. Refreshed and weightless in the morning he would shower erect and happy and amazed at his head, and he would go and guzzle half a can of orange juice from the pie-shaped hole in the can, standing with his hand on his hip in the falling coolness of the open refrigerator. He has not been smoking two months now.

Having stopped smoking with his new memory and isolated in the freakish ticking silence and the bluegreen madness of the ocean, he began a kind of brooding consideration of his life and his new obsession with the rock, now closer, the forbidding and barren gray-brown protrusion with the waves crashing against it sending fans of spray fifty feet into the air. In rhythm with the churning of his legs his mind chants the questions to itself, why the water, why the rock at the mouth of the bay. It is not danger itself. It is something else. He has begun to think of it as friction. Resistance. This is what he seeks in the surrealistic madness of the ocean. Resistance. Without it what else is there that you could call life? Somewhere along the line I have negated resistance. And reclaimed it now in the soft but infinitely powerful resistance of water. Chanting, forming the words into the black tube of his snorkel, he thinks, resistance and conflict. I have not felt like this in years. It was a frictionless rise, right up the line, you scratch my back I'll scratch yours. And now, in half-conscious and boyish daydreams he invites the shark, dreads it but secretly hopes for its attack, his thumb gently resting on the crude trigger of his spear. He knows he is defenseless if one comes at him yet he cannot turn back, knows he will push until something comes to him.

He thinks that his memory did it to him. After he stopped smoking, he started recalling the time when he was a boy on a piss-poor farm, his chin like numb putty from the cold, herding the cows from the barn to the watervat, chopping wood trembling with hunger, his hands numbly locked on the axehandle, shivering, still hungry at night, his body tensed up so much that in the morning his stomach muscles would ache. Although those days on that worthless farm were miserable, he remembers them now with an obsessive clarity, and he feels a funny sentimentality as if somehow those were better days. He thinks of the present with idle contentment, but above that in some loftier recess of his mind there lies a peculiar membrane of disgust.

At home after work he will sometimes sit, drink in hand, in his hip colonial living room and moodily regard the denim-clad crotch of his wife Emma. She will most likely read a magazine, her own drink sweating on the glasstopped table. He loves her. She is strong and attractive and slatternly. It is a kind of sexy laziness. He will sit, sniffing at the vague odor of sweet jungle decay which seems to hang in and around the house. His eyebrows will draw together and he will think; lazy, everything is too lazy. How did we get here? Why do you just sit?

He does not choose to seek excitement in the lights of Waikiki. Unlike his colleagues, who come to work on Mondays with stories about stewardesses and oriental beachgirls and hookers, Calder finds the attractive depths of moral depravity uninteresting. He has made his slips, but the adventure he would have expected never materialized. His latest was here, on a lunch period—a secretary who would lean over his desk delivering letters and memos, moving in a way which suggested to him a certain substantial mammary heft. It was lunch in her apartment, and after a series of ridiculously obvious mutual suggestions she was naked and hanging on his neck. No conquest. It just—happened, and that was it. And sitting, he can hardly remember it. He can remember with more clarity his first time at sixteen on wet and dead hay stubble in March at two in the morning, the moon casting his own shadow on the pale body of a girl a year older than him, a girl he had to fight a bigger kid to claim as his. He can remember being cold and bruised, and his shadow moving on her.

At work or at home or at lunch he would sometimes sit and find himself working his knees together and apart together and apart like a boy being denied the shuddering relief of the bathroom. Wrong, something's just—wrong. He would find himself sweating in his air-conditioned office, an air-conditioning system that he himself helped to design. Air conditioning, he thinks, trudging along in the water, slowing down now with deep breaths of satisfaction, air conditioning is the essence of the whole thing. But the water makes him shiver so hard that on the beach after being in for three hours he knows he will sit with the towel around his shoulders and tremble and he will remember again himself a boy trying to talk with a frozen chin, useless putty, remember the terrible itch after warming up leaning against the wood stove above the cherry-hot metal and rotating so as not to overdo one side. He can see the line of his life as forward movement without friction or resistance. How did he come to make so much money when he was not sure that in the last seven or eight years he actually did any work? There is only the nebulous, conglomerate picture of himself behind desk or shoulder to shoulder with the right friends in the apartments or town-houses near Hunter or down the street from . . .

He missed—his spear disappears off into the sand and he tenses himself up. A parrotfish, big. Missed by only an inch or so. He is secretly glad that he missed, because he would have been burdened by the fish and he wants to go to the rock. Outside of that, his freezer has five of them stacked and wrapped in foil, no more than a nuisance to Emma who prefers supermarket fish imported frozen from the Bahamas or California. This has always bothered him because he feels a strong pride about his fishing. Retrieving his spear is a matter of diving down fifteen feet and finding the little trench it made before getting covered by the sand. He grabs the spear out of the sand and slowly ascending, slides it back through the handle and catches its notched rear end in the surgical tubing sling which, attached to the crude handle, makes the primitive rubber tension that provides the spear's thrust. It is held in place by a simple trigger that binds it in the handle, cocked and ready to fire again. He has no use for the new, technological air guns because they make fishing too easy.

He chuckles into the snorkel, thinking of Emma. One night, almost as if inviting a conflict, he told her about the secretary. Fired up on his Scotch at midnight a week ago he talked away about freedom and restriction and about how she was so liberal about things like that and knowing he should keep his mouth shut because he didn't want to spoil anything, he fell into this almost experimentally pushy interrogation. "Well, suppose I went off now and again and found some girl—" And she, in that wise, blond frankness of hers, said well who am I to tell you what to do? What if I went out and found some . . . He went on with, well, I know how women are supposed to feel about this stuff and . . . Don't worry about me, she said. And he stopped then, thinking, very smart. Build a fence around a pony and he'll jump it and run. Take it away and he'll stay. Very smart.

So he told her, gave her a five-sentence, objective picture of what happened, and then stood there and waited calmly for whatever she had for him. She looked at the floor. "Oh I see, I see what—that's what you're getting at. Well, interesting, interesting." When he walked toward her, across the glass-shiny kitchen floor, she took a little step of her own, as if not aware of his existence but really evading him. So then she was crying to herself, and he cursed himself for letting her know, thought, now you've done it, now you've taken care of it. Six years. No children. How easy it would be for her now to just—the speculations raced through his head, sending a shudder of odd exhilaration through him.

"Only once?"

"Yeah," he said. And she thought about it.

Finally she threw her hands up as if in annoyance and said, "Ah what the hell, it's the twentieth century after all, just be careful, okay?" Then she went off to bed, leaving him standing there in the kitchen looking out the window at the silhouette of the house next door, a carbon copy of his own, squat and comfortable and dark, surrounded by the sweetly decaying plumeria trees.

When he went to bed ten minutes later, apprehensive and cautious, she was hot and lying there in the rumpled bed in her slovenly nakedness and latched onto him and breathed her hot breath on his face and pulled him down on her liquid and softly demanding body. And he looked at her and said, "What—what's the—" and then chuckled to himself in morbid amazement and gave in.

Calder takes very seriously what he is doing, even against the soft and reasonable protests of his wife, who will not go with him to the beach when he plans his excursions. He even enjoys her fear. The last time she went with him, along with some other people from work, they were all worried sick that he would not come back because he was gone for two hours. And Emma said, "It really scares me you know, please don't go out so far . . . you go out so far I can't even see you."

He looks down and nods when she says this, knowing that he will not be able to resist going even farther the next time.

"I just don't understand why," she said. "They don't either," and she poked her thumb over her shoulder. "There's some sort of a—a blindness I don't understand. You say you won't and you do." She held her shoulders up in a sustained shrug.

And he nodded and looked down at the sand. He cannot explain it yet, but is secretly warm inside that she should be afraid. But outside of that there is the gnawing shadow of an understanding suggesting itself—he almost sees something he doesn't like, that in his obsession for the rock there is a certain puerile and egotistical and boyish motivation. There is evidence that he is almost afraid to examine too closely. Once on a short excursion he lost his spear in a cave and foolishly went in after it, knowing that the ocean could decide to drown him in there. Fishing around reef caves was dangerous anyway because one slip, one moment of loss of concentration could mean being badly bruised or even knocked out on the coral, because of the dangerously unpredictable nature of the waves. In the ticking blackness of the cave he retrieved his spear and tried to return to the light and a wave came in and then some strange current, which played with his life for ten seconds while he fought off the powerful impulse to breathe. Finally the current released him and he sprung to the silver surface of the water and exploded coughing into the noisy air, and coughing his throat raw he went right into the beach and sat trembling on his towel, thinking, I almost died there, I almost did not come out.

And later, he had some people over as usual and told them the details of his scrape, not at the moment recognizing that he was romanticizing it somewhat. And Emma, wise, sloppy Emma, said, "See what John Wayne's done to my husband?" Everyone laughed, Calder the loudest, and in the awkward silence that followed he sat in a haze of warm shame, as if Emma had insulted him.

And he thinks, what *has* John Wayne done to me? He deliberately passes up a lobster, sees the black feelers peeking out from under a blob of dead coral. Maybe she is right. Some blindness I don't understand. More evidence: heading for this same rock a few weeks ago he found himself halfway, outside of the crashing breakers, and he felt frightened and happy and looked goggle-eyed at the fish and the sleepy, deadly eels and the rilled sand, thinking, this is far, this is way, way out. Nobody, nobody would—and he turned and saw something off in the distance. He raised his head out into the cold air and saw something protruding from the water and began to back away, muttering with fear into the snorkel. It turned out to be a boy. Local. There was another boy farther off, and when he realized this he moaned, sick of himself, and returned to the beach. Boys. It seemed to prove the dilettantish nature of his adventure. And it was the same day that he looked at the ominous rock off the bay and thought, all right, boys, there, I have to go there.

He slows down and thinks, yes, there is something hokey about this, about me. He is thirty-two, idly resisting the half-conscious impulse to consider himself somebody's Christ. Why? he thinks. All right, so let's find out. He is convinced that the ocean holds for him some personal secret that only making it to the rock will reveal.

There is Martin, too, one of the right friends to have, also from New York. He is the one who said to Calder, "You want St. Johns or Honolulu?" Martin now pokes fun at him, calls him Lloyd Bridges, that guy from the old underwater TV show, or sometimes he says at work: "Ask Jacques Cousteau over there . . . ." Calder resents Martin's joking, because he knows that the question of what John Wayne has done to him is important and touchy and personal. Emma, you wise bitch. You who look like a turn of the century New Orleans whore in the morning all hoarse and sexy, you are a wise bitch. How could he explain it to her? Resistance is life, therefore where there is none, then there is no life. The Human has purged resistance from his life. What would she say? Aw, up yours honey, come to bed. Those hot, enveloping thighs and the great squash of breast that seems in the process of running off her chest. They seem to negate him.

He stops and puts his head out of the water and scans the mountains, the beautiful dark mountains with their outrageously green peaks in the clouds. He slowly treads water, his jaw quivering with cold. Then he looks at the minute dots of the houses, the crawly feeling at the back of his neck. He is not alert, and in principle, if he were a fish he would be dead. Living in the ocean means for them remaining perpetually alert. Or the shark, living for him means constant movement or suffocation. The eel sits in his hole and waits in perpetual readiness. God. He looks scornfully at the houses nestled under the mountains and shakes his head and snorts, thinks of himself sitting in his hip colonial living room which is decorated to make a social chameleon of him, a place with no balls. He thinks, that is the most indecisive room I have ever seen.

"All right," he says into the snorkel. He looks at the rock, scanning the water near it for the black triangle of a shark's dorsal fin. Only four or five hundred yards. Today's the day. His fear and excitement balance each other out. No one can help him now. He knows he is foolish, that this is not necessary and if Emma knew, she'd probably call the rescue squad. He looks up again, his face whipped by the cold wind, thinking, god it's big. It rises fifty or more feet out of the water, a fractured cube, threatening and monolithic and raw. The water sloshes against it in huge swells and he knows he cannot get too close. He sees also that the water under him is forty or more feet deep, which means he cannot use his spear. In front of him and down the bottom goes, off into the frightening blue distance. He is cold, shivering now but all the time enjoying it with his tense belly and back and the shudders in the throat and jaw. With the water getting deeper and the rock looming and his eyes darting around in the limit of his vision for the shape of a shark, almost as if it is the shape of proof that he lives at all, thinks okay, Emma, okay, what do you say now? The plot is thickening, honey. We'll move the cameras in when he comes at you.

He thinks enfolded in the pastel silence of the water with the blue nothingness below him, once you get there what will it mean? Behind this a more threatening thought comes to him, as if he is grimacing at himself in the mirror—he really is hokey, he really is a boy. This is almost too much for him. Trudging along slowly with exhaustion approaching, it is almost as if the excursion is ruined. He is shivering but inside he feels hot with shame. He has had this thought many times before, but today it wells up like a wave in his mind and he cannot easily rid himself of it. He looks up and sees his magnif-

icent rock and now the fear begins to outweigh the excitement. Now the mask hurts his upper lip and the fins are
chafing his Achilles tendons and his throat is salt raw as if
someone has run a woodrasp down it. Now he is tired and
wonders if he should try the last few hundred yards. He looks
up and sees that the land jut at the mouth of the bay is actually
closer to the rock than his point of entry. He decides he should
head for it, the humiliating thought gaining ground in his
mind. Another time sonny. Tomorrow maybe. He hangs
exhausted in the water and looks down at the blue-gray nothingness of what must be sixty feet of water, hangs blank and
tired and thinks, tomorrow Lloydo, tomorrow Jacques. This is
enough. He is too far out. Jesus, he thinks, I got to get back in. I
really got to get back in. Head for the jut. He will have to go
through scary, unfamiliar territory.

But he does not go in. Hanging suspended in the water and
now a little angry he thinks, why waste it just because someone implies that you are an irresponsible fool? Nothing to lose
out here but doubt, boy. Sullenly biting down on the mouthpiece and disregarding the exhaustion that drags him down
he churns on toward the rock, grimly forcing himself on
despite the fear which now lies dormant somewhere,
shadowed out by his brooding anger at anyone or anything
which would influence him not to go as far as he goddamned
well pleased.

He is rewarded quickly. Off in the distance, against the soft
blue of the ocean, the reef around the rock begins to mate-
rialize like a photograph in a chemical solution. The reef is a
hundred yards into the ocean around the rock, and it seems
alive with fish, and scanning the picture whose clarity in-
creases steadily, Calder sees nothing indicating danger. It is
all beauty. It sends a shudder of excitement through him like
ponderous electricity. It is incredible — he has never seen anything like this in his life. The yellows and pinks and the fish in
schools and the fish alone, going on about their business. It is
as if he has crossed a desert and come out into a beautiful
town.

He spends ten minutes in a gawking, amazed inspection of
part of the reef before he decides to fish for a few minutes. In
his excitement he misses the first shot at a large parrotfish in a
hole and he stays down, looking into the hole with his body
inverted, and grabs for the rear end of his spear which lies

across a crevasse full of little silver fish. He almost has the spear when the spotted eel flashes on his hand. There is no pain, only momentary shock in which Calder even feels the eel's tongue on the palm and sees that its teeth are buried as far as they will go, and in that same, peculiarly objective expanded half-second he sees the little malevolent eye buried in the fat, bulbous head staring back at him sleepily. He jerks his hand out of its mouth so that the teeth painlessly shred the palm and back and he springs off the coralhead already taking water into his throat and he curls up around his shredded hand like a leaf in a fire. He rises to the surface blowing air from the snorkel in a yell and then hangs there waiting for the pain which does not come up beyond a cold and wretched discomfort. Wailing softly with each breath he looks at his hand. The slashes are closed with blood escaping in little billows, like smoke. He gasps his breaths numbed with fear and trembling wretchedly and clasps his hand to his chest, thinking, oh Jesus so far out, and blood escaping, Jesus.

Still without feeling much pain he turns and scans the water again and begins swimming backwards, frightened at the little billows of blood which disperse into the water. No defense, none at all. Get in. He looks up again at the jut of land, and rejecting the hollow fear of what must lie behind him and against his exhaustion he churns with all he has toward the jut. Before going two hundred yards he stops, gasping, cold and giddy and hopelessly tired. Before he can control it, bile scalds his throat and the inside of his nose, and he floats, eyes shut, trying to hold back the dreamy nausea which robs him of balance and strength. In order to keep from throwing up he hangs still, holding his hand against his chest, letting the ocean do to him what it will. For a moment he has a strange feeling, a strong impulse to just hang there forever, just die there enfolded in the water.

He needs to concentrate on something. Floating in aimless exhaustion is terrifying. He looks again at the hand, bringing it off his chest as if it were incredibly fragile. Still, the little billows, the seepage, and a kind of morbid interest in what the eel did makes him gently open one cut. It is even worse than he expects, like razors right into the muscles, all the way in, and the heel of his hand is partially severed, a one-inch chip in the flesh. He chokes with fear again and trudges on cautiously, because of his stomach, half-consciously muttering into the snorkel, Jesus god bad, my god my god, and he is too tired to glance back for the shark he is sure is on its way to finish the job. He can only chuckle with hopeless exhaustion and watch the rilled sand pass under him and curse with his teeth clenched when the ocean gently holds him back with one of its exasperating currents.

It is almost as if he sleeps, trudging along in the blue-green silence, as if he is at peace with his hand and now must simply go home. He has no idea how much time it takes him to make it any distance and he does not care. The fear has crystallized at the back of his head so that whatever feeling it is when some pair of jaws clamp on his neck will make him respond by simply drawing his shoulders up and wincing slightly. For long stretches he swims with his eyes closed, almost not caring if he is going in the right direction. His mind cocoons itself in a half-dream and it is only the growing pain that keeps him aware. Then the powerful breakers wake him up and carry him violently toward the shore so that he must raise his head out to get air. The sea is all foam, tossing him and pushing him and washing over him, all toward the beach, and he lies, his hand clasped to his chest, intent only on getting the air he needs when the ocean will permit it. Before reaching the calm water he has the wind blasted out of him by a high piece of coral that lays open the skin on his ribs. He continues on, a little hopeful because he is inside the reef, and the searing pain of the blow on his ribs wakes him up. And with horribly gradual progress, the bottom comes up to meet him.

On the shore he plows up to dry sand, still holding his hand, and falls back. He is almost too tired to keep going, but the recognition that he has made it to shore gives him a temporary energy and the noise of the land wakes him up and the blood streams from his hand because it is now not held in by the pressure of the water. With his good hand he pulls the fins off holding the bad hand aloft so that the blood runs down his arm over his elbow and toward his armpit. Gasping more air than he needs he is driven by a sullen fear as if something could still chase him and he begins trotting along the beach toward his car which is a mile away, and he fights the sand which slows him down.

A man intercepts him bearing a towel, which Calder numbly wraps around his hand, and the man leads him into the bushes saying. "Oh Jesus the bugger got you . . . oh Jesus . . ."

and Calder hardly hears him. It is as if Calder is still in the silent ticking ocean and numbly he follows staring glassy-eyed at his own feet in the sand and then on grass and finally wet and shivering and salty he finds himself sitting in the front seat of the man's car, holding his wrapped hand against his injured side.

The bleeding has almost stopped and blood crusts his wrist and forearm and soaks into the towel. Now he sees that the man is Japanese, old, and keeps glancing at Calder's wrapped hand. Calder looks around, at the ocean, and at the white line streaming into the hood of the car. It is as if he wakes up suddenly. He pulls the towel away and peeks at his hand. It is cupped against his side so that the seeping blood collects in the palm. He is suddenly apprehensive about going home, as if he were a boy who had injured himself doing something he shouldn't have done.

But he snorts angrily at that thought, and turns to the man. "Have you . . . have you ever been out there, by that rock?" His voice crackles, almost as if the question is urgent.

"Not for me," the man says, laughing.

"It's . . . it's beautiful," Calder says, "I've never seen anything like that in my life."

Now he is relaxed, calm, almost content sitting there hunched around his hand, and he thinks, against what reason would tell him to think, if this is the blindness they make it out to be, then I aim to keep it. He takes another look at his cupped hand and at the brilliant little pool of blood in the palm. He holds it as if it is something valuable he has found in the ocean.

The Rat's Eye

Our feelings about rats are not entirely rational. They are clean animals that spend long periods of time grooming themselves. Their fur smells almost sweet. If you look into their eyes, there is a certain angle where they seem like bottomless wells, of a black so deep as to become the suggestion of a vast and subtle light, like space. And so, amid the shrieks and rough laughter of gaudily dressed women and men in coveralls, I would know that biting the rats was not what it seemed to my audience. In recent times I only imitated the crushing bite on the back, and then, holding each one in my right hand tightly, my forefinger under the chin and my thumb locked securely against the back of the skull, I would kill them with a quick and merciful bite, my bottom teeth against their jawlines and the top neatly caving in the skull. My tongue would never touch the rat.

I used to carry out my act with snarling, bestial vigor. This was about six years ago, shortly after Mr. Bonham picked me up. Then I would stuff the rat back into my mouth and bite with all my strength, so that the animal's hair would lodge in locks between my teeth. The bite would break its lungs and blood would spurt from its mouth and onto my hands. Or I would wrench the body with my hands so that entrails would pop out of the mouth and bowels, and cast the animal out of the pit. There the mutilated animal would steam in the cool night air.

I will tell you how I became the principal attraction. It was due to the presence of the carny and to a life brutish enough that any excuse for escape would do. I grew up hating my father with a secret and intense passion. I dreamed for years of killing him under circumstances romantically just, and the dream went through years of refinement. We lived alone on a run-down farm in New York State back during a time when small farms just barely broke even. He hated cows, work, and schedules, as I did, but they had to be, and I was the whipping boy. It is not necessary to go into detail, except for one example: I have a pea-sized scar on my thigh, which came from the thrust of a shitty pitchfork on a day when my father, cautious lest he lose his slave, went to the barn and drove the fork into a cow's side and killed her.

One day we both went to the carny. He went to see the strip show and to drink with men he knew. I had never seen a carny, so I tried my hand at knocking down fur-fringed dolls and throwing rings at pegs. When we went home, my father yelled about my spending too much money and punched me in the face. I landed on the kitchen table, my hands in the sticky alcohol rings and pools of milk that never dried on that plastic cloth. I stood up, planning to hit him back, but lost the nerve and ran out.

I stowed away on the beef truck. This is the semi that hauls the carny horses Eveline uses in her act, and Hubert the Two-Faced Bull, a natural freak with two noses and sets of lips separated by a deep cleft. When I felt the truck stop and saw the door open to daylight, we were near Buffalo, having driven much of the late night. Mr. Bonham ordered me to get the hell away from his equipment, but I told him I wasn't going home and if he could find something for me to do I'd do it free.

"What can you do?"

"Any old thing, any old thing."

He was joined by Professor Tait, the magician and emcee. Tait was drunk. "How about making this shaggy-haired boy a geek?"

"Geeks are out," Bonham said. "Nobody believes in geeks these days." Thinking, he looked as if he were in pain. "You eighteen yet?" I had five months to go.

"About," I said. "What's a geek?"

"Why don't you go on home, kid?" he said. "I got no use for you."

"I ain't goin'," I said, folding my arms.

Bonham walked off. Tait stepped up. "This is a good sign, son. Let the man think."

Bonham always looked miserable as he watched over the various processes of his dilapidated carny. It was with this look of misery and uncertainty that he came back with his proposal, which I later recognized as partly a method of driving me off that failed. He kept muttering that they used to do this once, but not in a long time. I was eager enough that it meant nothing to me. I said why not. Bonham and Tait were both a little shocked. They turned away and mumbled. Tait seemed to advise against it. I thought the idea was awful too, but had no alternative.

Here I am, standing in my filthy jeans and lumberjack shirt while one of the drivers, swearing about having to drive twenty miles to find a town with a pet shop, comes up with the cage. "I don't know about this," Mr. Bonham says.

It was the forwardness and guts of youth. I'm not going to blanch. I take the cage with a shiny brown rat in it, really kind of pretty, with beady black eyes. While Bonham and Tait mutter their reservations, I take it out. I hold it steady, swallow, throw off that last little hesitation. I bring it to my mouth. The men look away, the rat struggles. Quick—I bite down on its spine and rib cage so hard that the bones crunch in a tiny explosion no one can hear but I can feel in my teeth, and with a quick squeal and wheeze the rat is dead.

"I don't know about this," Bonham says. "Years ago, maybe my own father with this outfit here. Could be. Could be even he did it. I just . . ."

It is a redneck's carny, small and cheap. You have Eveline with her horses, Hubert the Two-Faced Bull, the wire performers, modest rides. There is Denise Lovelace, the stripper. For the sideshow, Billy Young and his rats, and then the Armless Wonder, a man who only stays with us half the time, who can throw this great curve without anything four inches below either elbow—he holds the ball in the crook and wings it; he writes, does all kinds of stuff. There is good old Professor Tait with his magic act and his mind reading. There is the two-headed baby, a freak who has spent the last thirty some-odd years in a huge bottle of alcohol with a slowly swirling suspension of flecks of skin. The baby's eyes are puffed closed; it hangs there wax white, with its umbilical cord under its arm.

Bonham's way is to head for smaller rural towns and make a deal with a sort of well-known farmer to use some bit of pasture near a macadam road. Then it is a matter of putting the posters around, working two weeks ahead by sending useless old men out to do the PR work. The caravan of trucks, five in all, constitutes the carny packed up. The tents and equipment arrive early. Then come the beef and the performers, who do some rehearsing during mornings before the goonies come to blow their money. The performers sleep in motels, travel in cars. The lowlies, as we call ourselves, drive the beef and tents through the night, dazed and nodding at the beams of our own headlights bouncing on the road ahead. We stay three or four days in a town. Mr. Bonham is a clean man, and we have to pick up every shred before we vacate. He knows how people cheat, but does not intervene. He knows that Denise Lovelace discards her pasties and G-string to reward the drunks at the end of her act—serves herself up in poses illuminated by the beam of a flashlight held by Professor Tait, now drunk enough that his aim wavers, an error whose gravity he does not sense. Mr. Bonham knows that one of the beef men is a pickpocket, that Professor Tait is sometimes too drunk to do his magic, that Denise costs twenty dollars in off times.

My act is the center of the sideshow. Mr. Bonham is always scared that someone will holler, call the newspapers, the SPCA. He always looks at me with surprise on his face, as if he could never believe I had the guts.

All right, you are a consumer. You have seen the Borellis's wire act, Eveline, Hubert. You have shot the twenty-twos and your fingers stick together annoyingly from the remnants of the cotton candy. Now it is time for Billy Young.

Professor Tait emerges from a tent flap, grave and thoughtful.

"Ladies and gentlemen, I will dispense with loquacious formalities. Inside this tent is a boy, found by persons who wish to remain anonymous, up in the southern backcountry of Canada—Billy Young. No one knows how he survived, but survive he did, by predatory instinct. What you will see may shock you, but remember that he is acting according to behavior instilled in him before he could walk. He may appear to you to be simple, perhaps imbecilic, but in truth he is as intelligent as the wolf, as crafty as the fox or the bobcat. He is not dangerous. He is as kind and harmless as a baby. If he gazes at you, perhaps tries to touch you, do not be alarmed; his touch is as swift and gentle as that of a wild bird. But realize that what he is about to do is natural for him, no matter how horrible it may seem to you."

You are ushered into a little round theater with the pit down in the middle. The light is rich, yellow; the pit is a circular solid fence, three feet high. In the center is a dog's screw tether, twisted into the ground, with a chain disappearing into a box that opens into the pit. You sit above it on paintless bleachers.

Professor Tait stands on a platform above the pit, his expression serious, sad. The cone of light holds in it a suspension of dust and tobacco smoke. About one-third of the audience is women. The box door opens and out scrambles Billy Young, the chain around his neck, his muscular body darkened with bootblack, wearing a loincloth of sheepskin. He has been given heavy sideburns and patches of hair on his back. Cautiously, with a look of animal fright, he works the perimeter of his pit. "Yes, ladies and gentlemen," Professor Tait says in a sympathetic voice, "there he is, visitor and symbol of our distant past," and goes on with his speech, dropping in points of information about evolution from his dim memory of Darwin and from *Compton's Encyclopedia*, which he and I flipped through while working up and refining the pitch.

Billy stops, suddenly gazing with curious innocence and cautious lust at a woman's high-heeled shoe. She screams with delight and draws it back under her skirt and hides it in a wild arrangement of crinolines which resembles a giant carnation. Billy Young looks sad, as if he will cry. He reaches out with a tentative and halting quaver toward the vision of that vanished shoe. She screams again, frightening him into an animal flinch. He cowers, confused. He patrols the perimeter of his pit, catches the eye of an old man, hunches with primitive shame. Looking back, he growls low in his throat, suspicious.

Professor Tait opens a small trapdoor and in come rats, caught earlier in the day or yesterday at the town dump or the GLF feed store. Billy scrambles to the center of the pit as the rats herd along the perimeter, frightened by noise and light into spastic jerks, jumping against each other with nerves electrified by confusion. The audience gasps—diseased and vile, the rat, representative of all that is horrifying in nature. An animal of such uselessness and destruction—they all have stories about raided grain bins, eggs filched from chicken coops, bites on children. But more important is the aura of evil rats possess. Billy looks at them with hunger and a deep and ancient hatred. He stalks one, expertly homing in on it, cornering it, confusing it with his hands, which move with catlike speed and grace. The rat is caught. It squeals, a loud and high-pitched scream. He looks at it with dumb interest, makes as if to pet it with smug affection. It is locked securely in his right hand, struggling, trying to turn its head to bite. Billy carries it to the perimeter and offers it, his face melancholy with desire, to the lady of the shoe, and she screams again, backed by harsh laughter. Billy winces and is made angry by the rejection. Shamed, he sulks, looks at the rat. Miserable in his disappointment, he seems to think, to consider where the blame lies. Then suddenly he stuffs the back of the rat into his mouth and crushes it with a single bite, so that blood spurts from its mouth and runs in a single bright stream down his forearm. He puts the head in his mouth and crushes the skull, then looks up with a satisfied, sensual leer at the screaming lady, grinning at her with bloody teeth. The crowd roars with horror and appreciation. Women cover their faces. Billy turns, casting the dead rat aside. He slowly tastes the blood, and a new expression crosses his face, one of single-minded lust. He looks, interested. Six more rats cower on the other side of the pit, sniffing, the black beads of their eyes reflecting the light from the lamp above.

The first night we would do one show. The second we would have to do two, each time to a packed tent. Mr. Bonham saw it only once and then went back to his trailer and got drunk. My act put him far in the black and kept him there for all the time I traveled with the carny, even though fear of the SPCA frequently made him cancel the show. Even so, he kept me at a distance and did not seem to like me. Nobody did. I was tainted.

I loved the traveling. We would have two or three days off a week usually, and after Professor Tait became friendlier to me we would go into town and look in the library. He was a man of maudlin and pessimistic curiosity. He wanted to read papers, see magazines, hunt with sad-eyed diligence for certain books. My reading was slow at first, but I got better, to the point where I would read a book in a day—some of my own choosing, like the works of Max Brand and Owen Winter, and some difficult and mysterious books recommended by the professor. The professor and I talked a lot, but rarely about my job. When that subject came up, it was always from the edge. Once he shifted gravely in his seat and took a slug from his bourbon flask and told me a story about rats. He described something he'd read in a book, about some rats in a nest above this big box, with a tennis ball covered with meat juice in the bottom. One rat crawled down the wall and sniffed the ball, decided it was worth taking back to the nest, but could not push it up the wall. Soon he went to the nest and came back with another rat. One rat wrapped himself around the ball and the other grabbed his tail in his mouth and dragged him and the ball up the wall and into the nest.

"My boy," he said, "you bite an animal of some craft."

"No shit," I said. The story did not impress me at the time. In the library I was interested only in rats' diseases and read *Compton's* on the plague, rat-bite fever, tularemia, typhus. Being reckless, I concluded that I was okay as long as I did not swallow during the act and used the Listerine after.

From Buffalo to Binghamton, into Pennsylvania and the Appalachians, in the winter into North Carolina, we ground on with our old trucks, sending men ahead to spread the word. Near urban areas my act was canceled as the threat of SPCA spies haunted Bonham's imagination. One time he appeared at the beginning of a show to hand-signal me into faking the whole thing, to fake the bite and cast the unharmed rat back into the cage. He was always afraid of the law, of suits and fines. Nevertheless for me the whole thing was colorful and exciting, the feeling of movement was in my blood. Every day we had restaurant eggs in the morning and fried chicken the rest of the time. A few times I was lucky enough to become involved with women.

The beginning of the change came after about four years. I had become used to our movements, returns to key places, and the hiring and firing of performers, whom we lowlies did not associate with much. In fact, it was the possibility of such an association that started it. I liked this girl Maria Bertini, touring with us as part of a tumbling and wire act from Italy. I would watch her doing her act up in the higher cone of the tent, swinging lean and muscular with powerful thighs and indented silver buttocks. Another performer in that group — her boyfriend, I guess — noticed this and confronted me after one of their daytime practices. He came to me smiling and suddenly decked me with a punch to the side of the head. He laughed, insulting me in Italian. When I got up, he hit me again. Bonham broke it up. He was angry at me. My head ached for days and I had strange dreams.

Three nights later, still achy in the head, I was on my third rat, snarling and biting its back. I overdid it, because on that bite, egged on by the howls of the audience, I tore the skin off its side, something like pulling a glove off, turning it inside out on the way. In the bright light, in that suspension of dust and smoke, I looked down at what I held in my hand and there, steaming in the cool October air, was the slick musculature of the rat. The vision shocked me, so that my eyes were glazed. At that moment my guise as beast must have vanished too, because the audience became silent. Still quivering slightly, the rat glistened in the light, little strands, almond shapes folded over other shapes, the incredibly delicate and complex front leg crisscrossed by tendons and thin ribbons of muscle.

The act continued. That night, however, I could not sleep, though sleeping had never caused me any trouble. I dozed for a while and got up before dawn, planning to occupy myself with useful work. But that vision from last night was troubling, for reasons I could not figure. I had seen inside the rat, and something about its complexity bothered me. Standing there in the near-frosted air, the dawn faintly showing in the sky, I stared at the dying blackness where the faded stars accentuated the frightening distance you sense in that almost-light. I concluded that, if anything, this curious worry was Maria Bertini's fault.

We moved on. Next stop was Buffalo and one last hustle before winter and the South. It was like fate was on my heels. Only a week after skinning the rat I bit the back of one, the seventh and last of that night, and my bite missed, so that the rat bore three of its young into my lap. There, steaming and moving slowly with life, they looked like blue-gray bullets, leaving trails of slime and membrane between themselves and their dead mother. Again the crowd shrieked and went silent, and I was unable to continue for a good twenty seconds.

Professor Tait noticed the gradual change after this. Now I did not attack the rats with the old vigor. My beast now bit them with a kind of delicacy. He raises the rat, offering it to the lady of his choice with grave formality. He seems unconcerned about her rejection, as if he has been expecting it all along. When it comes time for the bite, he fakes crushing the rib cage and uses his thumb and forefinger to hold it steady for the skull crunch, the first real pain inflicted on the victim. That bite creates an eruption of energy in his teeth so that he feels the ripple of reverberation through his jaw. He spits into the dirt rather than tasting the blood lustfully. Then he turns to the rest, sullen and thoughtful.

The consequence was that only one show was necessary,

and the tent was not packed, the shrieks not as loud. Bonham blamed it on the weather. Tait and I knew.

I fought my growing self-consciousness by gritting my teeth and deliberately trying to resurrect my old beast, but it didn't work. I would become jittery before the act, had trouble carrying through. I would hunker, sweating, in the box while Tait loudly ad-libbed an elongated introduction, until he would rap the box with his fist. The gibes of the audience hurt me. At the library the magnetic force of my problem drove me to read up on rats—I was astounded by the information that rats can fall from great heights without injury, can virtually collapse themselves so they are small enough to fit through a hole the size of a nickel, can swim for hours in icy water without freezing. Though our greatest pests, we cannot beat them. Reading this opened the door upon a multitude of deep questions—men and animals, natural aberrations, evolutionary history, the future. I flipped through the encyclopedia, reading up on them all. I also became fascinated by Bonham's two-headed baby, to the point where I would find myself standing in deep contemplation of it for long periods of time, speculating on its past, on its victimization by nature, on who it would have been. During the day a shaft of light would sometimes pass through the jar, illuminating the fine suspension of material in the alcohol and making translucent the waxy yellow skin of its fingers and the layer of fine sediment in the bottom of the jar. I would leave feeling insignificant, without substance or meaning, old and mortal.

In the van one day, hearing the incessant scratching of rats left over from last night—those which were not used because there was no need for a second show—I took one out of the cage and held it while Professor Tait drove. As it looked up at me sniffing, frightened and limp, I noticed its eyes. When the sun hit at a certain angle I saw a hole in which a peculiar light shone, but in reverse, as if I were the light and it flashed into the rat's head. There in that sunlight, leaning closer and closer, annoyed at the bumps in the road, I saw into it—the almost-light, the infinity, as if its eye were the convex doorway into another universe.

I put it back. Professor Tait pulled out his flask. "I know what's bothering you," he said.

"Ain't nothin' botherin' me." I said, flushing. I was ashamed about it, especially about his knowing.

"Well," he said, "have a drink with me, will you?"

"I don't drink," I said. "And there ain't a goddamn thing wrong."

"C'mon, have a little swig. Make you feel better."

He handed me the bottle, and I drank.

Dawn was the worst. Whenever I got up because of those sleepless nights — and a whole series of these nights hit me in waves over that year — I would wander out over the trampled grass and ride-ticket stubs and flattened cotton candy cones, and I would look up into the sky and see that near-light and recognize that it was the same as the light in the rat's eye, that faint suggestion of dawn, of vast and subtle light confined in the tiny skull. And I would sometimes wander to the sideshow tents, and there, pale and sort of spectral in the morning light, the baby floated in its alcohol, now thirty-seven years old.

We were near Hale Eddy, in Pennsylvania. I got out of my cot, hearing the faint scratching of the rats. In the black night the trucks were grouped, glistening dimly with dew, and into the sky came the beginning of dawn. I went to the van and looked in on the rats. One climbed the wire. The others were piled in the corner, either sleeping or keeping warm. I gathered my possessions and the money I had saved from my small salary. I went over and knocked on the professor's door, but could not wake him. He was too drunk. I went back to the truck in the advancing light and pulled the cage out, and carried it to a culvert near the road. There I opened the little wire door and watched them gradually explore their ways out, nervous and sniffing, and disappear with soft squeaks into the culvert and freedom.

"What are you doing?" It was Mr. Bonham, standing there with a flashlight which was of no use now in the sunrise. He turned it off. "Good weather again," he said.

"I want to explain about . . ."

"You don't need to, Son," he said, and mused, scratching his chin. "The professor told me. We'll keep you as a barker."

"I think I'll stay here a couple days, maybe a week, and then catch up. I'll hitchhike."

"Sure," he said. "Fine. There'll always be a place."

It was time to pack the trucks for a short hop to another town. When Tait got up, Bonham talked to him. I went over to tell them I'd take maybe two weeks. When I joined them they stopped talking. Tait cleared his throat. "Well, I hear you're taking a vacation after all these years."

"A short one. No big deal."

"Well, let's have a little drink to—well, to give you a proper send-off."

"It's early in the morning."

"Hell, it's after seven," he said, winking at Mr. Bonham. They chuckled over that. We had the drink, out of his flask. Bonham wiped his mouth and handed me the bottle, and I was shocked at the familiarity of the gesture.

Later, sitting near the culvert, I watched the carny move on, the trucks top-swaying along the road, followed by the small one in which sat Tait and Bonham, now a little drunk from the repeated good-byes, repeated jovial backslaps and hand-shakes. I thought their reaction to my vacation was absurd. The last I ever saw of them was when Bonham opened the door for the professor and said,"Here, ride with me," and Tait said, "Why, thank you, sir," and Bonham said, "Yessir, another fine day," and got in.

Now I work on a farm so large that I herd cows with a jeep. In the summer as I tool along cutting the hay I sometimes scare up deer, and they bound over the fences, their white tails up. I get up early and go out to the jeep in the near-light, and set woodchucks to running as I pass. Sometimes carnies stop near town, and I do not go. When they are there I become nervous and at night my heart thumps me into sleeplessness, and I always pause a long time before I turn the key in the morning and look into that near-light in the sky, which I first discovered inside the rat's head, sitting there that time in the truck all dumbfounded and thoughtful next to Professor Tait.

Light and Power

The first time Nathan Beech tried turning his lights off when he saw the Light and Power car coming up the long, winding road toward his home, he almost fell off the pole and came very near to electrocuting himself. He knew he had almost two minutes in which to complete the job, but actually doing what he had so thoroughly rehearsed made him tremble almost uncontrollably as he climbed the pole. But he was confident the next time they came, on a Tuesday afternoon two weeks after their first visit. He knew that if the Light and Power man was coming at all, he would come either on a Monday or Tuesday afternoon, and they were on schedule as he had expected. He got up quickly from his chair, put on his rubber gloves and nodded hastily, ran out of the house and across the lawn to the pole. It was easy to climb, and as he went up, he thought that he was in good shape, being forty and able to get to the top of the pole in a matter of seconds, in fact, before the car was one-fifth of the way up the hill. From his perch by the transformer at the crossbar, he could see all the way into town, and he scanned it once and drew out his pliers and quickly removed the copper eye of the 110-volt wire from the slot on the transformer. The lights in the house went off, and he heard his mother call.

"Okay," he yelled, making his way down the pole. "I'll see what it is!" But he knew that wouldn't satisfy her, so he went to the front door, figuring the time it would take to smooth her over and get back out to the Light and Power man in time.

When he knocked, she called him in. She was perched on her bed, her white eyebrows forming a wide V on her wrinkled forehead, and when he stood at the foot of the bed, she sighed heavily.

"Tell them Light folks somethin's wrong up here, will you?"

"Fuse, I 'magine," he said, and she looked at the little radio on the night table beside the bed.

"Well," she said, tipping her head toward it, "I lost my program again . . . that's the second time."

"Don't worry, I'll get it fixed," he said, and she smiled. He nodded, even bowed slightly to her and turned and left quickly, thinking that the car would be in the driveway. It was, and the Light and Power man, a new one this time, a small and sinister looking one, asked Beech for the money, got his answer and left inside of a minute. When the car disappeared down the road, Beech climbed back up the pole, took out his pliers, and whistling a march tune, hitched the looped copper end of the 110 wire back on the slot on the transformer. The lights in the house blazed on. It was as easy as that.

Spring was the year's weakest link for anybody who depended on the soil for an income. Beech shipped only one and a half cans of milk a day, but as far as he was concerned it was enough, and in order to operate his farm properly, he had to keep such things as electricity available at all times. He also needed it because his mother, who was now eighty and practically bedridden, had to be fed and had to have her radio to keep her busy. Keeping her busy was keeping her alive, in his way of thinking. So on Mondays and Tuesdays he would spend the afternoon in his living room. From there he could see cars coming from at least a mile down the long dirt road that ran to Jordan. In order to get the lights off in time, he had to see them coming the minute they turned off the highway to begin winding up the hill. Luckily, his mother spent these hours in her bedroom with special radio programs, and he wasn't bothered by her.

He had told the Temple County Division of the New York State Light and Power Company that he would pay them later, from the income he made on his potato crop. There was always a market for them, but no, they wouldn't listen. It wasn't security enough for them. He could hold them off for just a short time, and then they got tired of his promises to pay his bill and sent the serviceman up to turn off the lights. And when Beech's mother would listen to no more of his promises to get the Light and Power people to fix the "faulty system," he took it into his own hands and ventured up the pole.

Beech knew he would have to bend a few of the rules to keep the place running until summertime. He figured he wasn't cheating the Light and Power Company now because he knew he would pay them when he got his potato money. In his way of thinking, he was wrong only in that he kept his deal a secret. It was like the agreement he had with his neighbor, John

Summerhill, who had rented fifty acres of Beech's best pasture earlier in the spring and put off payment until summer. As of April twenty-first, Summerhill owed Beech almost fifty dollars, but because Beech knew these were hard times, he didn't pressure Summerhill for the money. He respected the promise to pay, and thought that the Light and Power people, who had gotten his business for years, at least owed him the same favor.

Beech simply would not go back to operating in darkness, because he knew it would lead to worse things, to giving up and selling his land and working for someone else as his father had to before the war. Beech was forced to take over when his father was killed in a chopper accident while working on a farm just outside of Jordan. His mother, a fragile woman, he figured, could not be left unprovided for. From the time of his father's death until he picked up where his father left off with their own farm, he worked for Summerhill in order to support himself and his mother. During that time, she sat down for good, but was still active, did most of the housework by wheelchair with brooms and dusters attached to long handles that Beech had fixed up for her.

They had installed the electricity about ten years ago, just after he had built up a running dairy farm again. Against his mother's wishes, he threw out the old Home Comfort stove that took up most of the space in the kitchen, got the appliances one by one and strung wires throughout every building on the place. By that time electricity was practically a necessity—there were other farms around Jordan that were run without electricity, and they were objects of general store conversations, local jokes. They were backward.

The future improvements he had planned, barn cleaners, stainless steel milkhouses, like the ones he had seen and read about and daydreamed over so many times in *Successful Farmer*, were not for himself only as he saw it. He wanted all his improvements to be made before his mother died. That was his deadline, and he could not overlook the fact that she had not much time left—perhaps ten years. It would take him about ten years to carry out his plans. It was important to him that she live to see it, and that he be there to see her skepticism of his years of talking and planning melt away. The Light and Power business was just a stone in the road to success.

"It'll be all right as long as I keep them fuses goin'," he told her the third time it happened, and he was glad again that they didn't have a phone.

"Well," she said, wheeling herself quickly down the hall to the kitchen, "That's what happens when you gotta depend on people you never see. . . ."

"That's the way it is today," he said.

"If the Germans ever . . ."

"The Russians."

"Well, I don't like it."

"It's more convenient than using wood for heat and milking by hand."

"When you gonna get a woman in here to use all this truck?" she asked, looking angrily at the gleaming appliances.

"Look," he said, "this farm wouldn't be worth a tinker's damn without lights. Nowadays, everything's electric."

" 'Lectricity don't make alfalfa grow," she said.

"But it keeps food in our mouths, puts hay in the barn," he said, and then she gave in.

"I suppose," she said, and smoothing her white hair back over her ears, she nodded. "Guess I wouldn't have the radio either."

"Right," he said, and she was silent. With the end of that discussion, he felt relieved that things would go well until the Light people came again.

But things didn't go well—Wednesday, bad news came. Morgan, the man who ran the milk truck that carried Beech's milk to the processing plant, brought it. "So that's it," he said. "I cannot afford to come up here for just one or two cans. It takes fifteen minutes to get up the hill, and must use about a gallon of gas. It isn't worth it."

"But I don't have a car or truck," Beech said, growing hot from Morgan's last sentence. "What the hell can I use to get it there?"

"Get a truck," Morgan said.

"Come every two days."

"Can't do that . . . day old milk ain't really legal on the long-term basis as far as I know, and still it wouldn't be worth it. Can't you get more stock?"

"Yes, yes, that's what I'll do. I'll do that, you keep comin'," Beech said, flushing, "You do that . . . keep comin'."

"Well, I'll come day after tomorrow and see how things are goin'," Morgan said, and he left Beech standing by the loading dock, and Beech turned quickly and shoved his hands down in his overall pockets. He decided that he wouldn't tell his mother, that he would have to do something and that it would have to be right away. When a man made the decision to thrash to shore rather than drown, he didn't quit just because of a widening river or a waterfall.

He couldn't keep his heart from thumping heavily when Morgan came into the driveway two days later. He stood leaning against the loading dock, three cans of milk by his right shoulder. Morgan nodded and smiled approvingly.

"Well," he said, "back in business, eh?"

"Yep," Beech said, helping him get the cans on the truck. "And it ain't two days old, either."

"Was afraid of that, but I'll take your word for it. Where'd you get the cows?"

"Had 'em right along," Beech said, laughing, "jest didn't know where the sonsabitches were hidin'."

" 'S long's you got it, I'll come up after it," Morgan said, and got into the truck and left. Beech watched him go down the road, the cans rattling heavily on the back of the truck, and he rubbed his eyes and yawned. He figured he'd better get used to getting up earlier, because he would have to do it every night until he built up his herd. And this was the only way he could get enough money to buy more stock.

The alarm woke him again at two in the morning, and he had an easier time getting up. He sat silently on the edge of his bed and listened until he heard the steady breathing from the other bedroom, and he moved quietly, hardly hearing himself dress. He made no noises in the barn either, and when he was finally ready to go, had his two milk cans wrapped in burlap bags and his pail slung over his shoulder, the rope halter and the pocket full of grain, he edged quietly out of the back door of the old barn, into the high thick grass that grew between the barn and the woods. It was cold in the woods, and it took him fifteen minutes to work his way there, systematically holding his direction through the motionless blackness of the air and out into the pasture he rented to John Summerhill, to collect his money's worth for the unpaid rent. He had decided that it was necessary to take this liberty and that it was justifiable because Summerhill owed him the money and was pasturing the cows on his land.

He could just make out the small black silhouette that was

Summerhill's house and barn, and when he did he held the cans and pail tighter to keep them from making the slightest noise. He put them down behind one of the thick maples that lined the pasture and quietly tiptoed toward Summerhill's herd, checking all the time for glints of light from the house, and all the way he soothed the cows, held his hand out cautiously, even made his expression gentle and moved slowly, inched on tiptoe toward them without jerking his hands or feet. And they noticed him, some edging toward him and some away, and the more inquisitive ones sniffed and looked at him with dumb interest. This Jersey, he thought, was the first one last night. He looked up and saw some of the other ones he had picked, the more docile, easier milkers. It was easy. He slipped the old rope halter over her head, pulled a little grain out of his pocket and led her to the tree. The ones that were finished as time went on, five in all by the time he started the last cow, watched from various distances, and there were no noises at all except the first drum of the milk on the bottom of the pail and of it pouring steaming into the cans. When the milking was done he had one and a half cans, and he took a half hour getting back, lugging the cans twenty or thirty feet at a time and resting in the blackness, leaning against trees and sitting in the soft leaves until finally the dim outline of his barn showed through the trees. When he finally got to bed it was four-thirty.

"Pork chops, eggs, hamburger," John Summerhill said, checking the weekly list of Beech's groceries, "beer and . . . Jesus, I don't know," he said, scratching his chin. He sat down on the running board of his truck. "It seems like it might be some of them old apples. Does apples do that to them?"

"Bujesus, I don't know," Beech said, shaking his head and looking up to the top of the light pole, then to his watch.

"How's yourn?"

"They're all right, gone up as a matter of fact," Beech said.

"Dropped two whole cans . . . thing that bothers me is that the others might ketch it," Summerhill said. "Maybe it's weeds."

"Mebbe."

"I'm gonna get rid of 'em, all six."

"Oh, I wouldn't do that," Beech said, but too quickly, and he flushed, paused and calmed down. "After all," he said, "it's spring. They might pick up after a while. You never know."

"Think it might be disease? It's just like they been milked clean. Jest about empty." Summerhill shrugged.

"Might be—never know."

"Listen, about that rent," Summerhill began, standing up.

"Fergit it," Beech said. "I know you can't pay it now. Hard times. We can let it go for now." Summerhill nodded with an absent stare and left. Beech watched him disappear down the road, then looked up at the transformer on top of the pole. He had spent most of the afternoon in the living room because either that day or the next, sometime in the afternoon, the Light and Power people might be visiting. Just as he got settled in his living room chair he saw them. But it was a truck, and he ran out trying to think of why they would send a serviceman. He thought that they must have read the meter, and he climbed the pole to the transformer and looked out and down the hill. The dust was one-fifth of the way up the hill, and he unhitched the wire quickly, heard his mother bellow from her bedroom, called to her that it was that damned fuse and got down from the pole, muttering frantically to himself. He tried to remember how the wire was when he first hitched it up but couldn't, and he stood at the bottom of the pole like a soldier at attention when the truck came into view again. He tried to compose himself, but his heart thumped harder when the truck came into the driveway.

He stood with his hands shaking in his pockets while the serviceman looked the meter over, climbed the pole, fiddled with the wire by the box and came down again.

"Somebody's been foolin' with that," he said to Beech when he was down again. "Any wise kids around?"

"Might be, Beech said, relaxing and taking his hands out of his pockets. "Lots of 'em just over the hill there," and he made an uncertain gesture behind him.

"Well, there was some tape on that wire and it's gone," the man said, scanning the woods Beech gestured at, and Beech thought a second, nodded, scratched his chin.

"Bad weather up here," he said, pointing up. "Mighty rough weather."

After that, the serviceman took out the meter, looked it up and down and muttered something about kilowatts, put it back in the pole and attached a new wire seal on the meter brace. Then he left. Beech stood and looked blankly at the new obstacle, deciding that it was a little too complex and began walking toward the house, going over what he would say to his mother. At the door he stopped and changed his mind and went back to the pole.

After hitching the wire back on the transformer, and placing the new tape on top of the transformer, he got down and went to the meter. It was on a lucky impulse, his decision to concentrate on that—after breaking the little wire seal near the brace where the break would be difficult to find, he fooled with the meter, looked over the four copper prongs on the back. Within ten minutes he had it back in the pole upside down, his electricity back and no registering of kilowatt hours in the meter. In order to be ready for the Light and Power folks this time, he had to unhitch the wire from the transformer, put the tape back on the end and reinsert the meter upright again. He just had to be a little faster.

It occurred to him frequently that all he was doing wasn't making him progress any further. He had to figure out how to get some more stock, and only money would do that. He was getting tired of sneaking around in his own pasture, climbing the pole, feeling like a criminal in his own front yard. It would have to end soon. Then it hit him.

"How're those cows?" he asked Summerhill the next time he came to Beech's house for the grocery list.

"Same," Summerhill said.

"Just thinkin'," Beech said slowly, "I know some of that vetternary stuff. Mebbe I could do somethin' with 'em."

"I had them Buchanan vets up already," Summerhill said, "and they told me there wasn't nothin' wrong with them cows. Said they was just gone mostly dry."

"I'll buy 'em from you," Beech said.

"What?"

"Just what I said. I'll buy 'em. They ain't doin' you no good now, so maybe I can do somethin'. Change the pasture. Maybe it's weeds, like you say."

"C'mon, Nate, you ain't got the money right now, and I ain't got it to buy more stock . . . . "

"No money," Beech said, moving closer and lowering his voice to near a whisper. "Just about five acres per cow. That oughtta be about right, I guess, hadn't it?" Summerhill threw his head back and laughed.

"You're crazy," he said. "I'd be takin' you for a ride."

"You've got forty head, and I've got more land than that barn'll ever handle. Seems right to me."

"Five acres?" Summerhill said, and he laughed again. "I'd always figgered you to be a little more shrewder'n that."

"Well," Beech began, and Summerhill cocked his head at him. He knows, Beech suddenly thought, trying to hold down his fright. "You think about it," he said slowly, and Summerhill shrugged and got into his truck.

"How's yours doin'?" he asked.

"Not so good . . . maybe they's gettin' that bug, too, I don't know." Summerhill looked at the sagging barn and smiled.

"Well, we'll see," he said, and left. He just doesn't want to say anything yet, Beech thought. But when he considered it further, he decided that it was probably his own fear that made him see it that way. Nevertheless, he decided that he would let the cows recover if Summerhill didn't sell within three days. What Beech was hoping was that Summerhill would come up the next night with the decision to sell already made.

But for the next three days he didn't hear from Summerhill, and he played it the same, got up every morning at two and carried the burlapped milk cans through the woods, milked the same cows, passed three cans of milk to Morgan every morning. Summerhill was to come up after the grocery list on the fourth day.

He was well set for the Light and Power folks when they came again. Before they got there he got a good idea and rested a shovel against the pole right near the broken seal wire, so that if they discovered it, he could say the wire was hit by the shovel. Having to climb up the pole and unhitch the wire, carefully put the tape back on, come down and turn the meter upright again and wipe his fingerprints off made it a little close for him. When he saw the car, with two men this time, he was just putting his handkerchief back into his pocket. There was one serviceman and the suspicious-looking little bill collector. They snooped around, checked the disc in the meter, climbed the pole. The little man acted strange about all of it, especially when Beech said, "Matter of fact, there were some sneaky lookin' people around the woods Friday." But they left and he was safe for at least another week.

Later that afternoon, when he had the lights back on again, his mother asked him outright if he was doing anything sneaky or illegal. She said she smelled something fishy. Even when he reassured her, she went on asking questions with an air of suspicion about his business dealings. With that short discussion he knew she was too close. He had to end it soon, and he knew he could safely when he got his milk check, which was due sometime shortly after Summerhill's next visit. He had to consider his mother first, so he decided that at some fixed date, no matter if things swung his way or not, the cows would have to make an exceptionally fast recovery, perhaps over a three-day span. That would reduce the chances of her finding anything out.

His main worry now was that if she found out, she would have a quick stroke and die, he was sure. He began to imagine her death in different ways, with different people bringing the news that would kill her. He imagined himself trying to answer for it, trying to explain away his responsibility. By the time Summerhill came again he had gone over it a hundred times.

Then Summerhill decided to hold off with the selling. He said that he was going to let them go and figure they just dried up for a while, maybe from some weed or some organic reason, and if nothing happened by summertime, he would get rid of them. Beech tried in vain to persuade him not to do that, that it would be better to see if he could do something with them right away, and Summerhill acted as though it would take too much time and effort to do it.

That night Beech crossed the fence into the pasture with only one can wrapped in burlap, the halter, pail, and grain. He had some trouble getting them over the knoll near the fence, and the first one kicked him. "Sure," he muttered, "because it's the second to the last goddamn, lousy stinking night ... sure ...."

When he had milked the first one two-thirds of the way, he turned to the rest, who stood in the gray moonlight, looking stupidly in his direction as he crept noiselessly. Why don't you just give up and come over here, you little bitches, he was thinking when another came up over the knoll. He crept closer and saw the silhouette of the widely spread horns of the seventh, muttered "Holstein," and stopped. As he squinted at it, it seemed a foot or more higher than the others, and he rose without thinking of being seen, even uttered a strained squeak before it pawed the ground once and charged. He sprinted toward the maple, and the rhythmic thudding of the bull's hooves came closer, gained on him. He almost had to dive headlong over the fence. The bull stopped and stood there a moment, looking at him as he drew breath, and Beech panted and thought in quick jumbles, he knew, the son of a bitch knew and put it there. "Tried to kill me, he did," he muttered softly, imagining Summerhill's sinister smile as it must have been when he settled down to a full night's sleep. He turned and looked into the woods and gritted his teeth. Why that miserable dirty rat, he thought, and he decided flatly that he would not give in—he would play the thing out as he had planned, just so Summerhill wouldn't feel he had won. He stayed much longer this time, until the sky lightened and he could see the brownish colors in the leaves in the woods. When he got home it was six o'clock.

The milk check was about three days overdue when the Light and Power man came again, but this time he didn't want to snoop. He told Beech that they knew what he was doing and that they were turning the lights off from another part of the line, down near the highway. When Beech remained cool and told him that he would pay them in a couple of days the man laughed at him. "Well, we don't really know if we can turn 'em on right away," he said. "Maybe in a couple of weeks or so, huh? In fact, we won't really be able to get up here for more'n a month. Might be August." He shook his head gravely and then smiled, spat in the dirt by the pole.

"We'll see about that," Beech said. "I'll go down to Buchanan and see your boss, how's that?"

"Say, I'd be mighty grateful if you did . . . he'll have me in for a fat raise, gettin' you in front of his desk." He stepped to the running board of the car. "Hah," he said softly, eyeing Beech with a knowing squint. Beech wanted to break the little man's neck, but he held himself steady.

"Well," the man said, spitting again, this time uncomfortably close to Beech's foot, "you get that money paid, hear? We might give you back your lights sometime."

"Sure," Beech said, shaking his head and clenching his fists at his sides, and the man left. Just for good measure, he figured he'd get all he could from the cheap sonsabitches and turn the lights back on again, and he did, quickly, almost falling off in his clumsy anger. He imagined getting his hands on the little Light man and soaking him once or twice in the manure gutters, ducking his head and throwing him off the place, or dumping two or three cans of rotten milk or watery summer manure on his car seats. Over all of it he worried about what would become of him, if they would press charges or investigate thoroughly, question the people in town, his mother.

When he explained to her that they might have to turn the lights off for quite a while in order to fix the system, she just eyed him sharply. He got away from her without too much hemming and hawing, and went on to the evening chores worrying about what processes of the law were working against him, and he hoped now that he could just scoot through it all without her finding out the whole story— suspicion was all right, but knowing everything, he was sure, would do all to her that his fantasy constructed.

Before the alarm rang at two in the morning, he had a dream about being shot while sneaking in the pasture. It was a large Summerhill who did it. The figure aimed and laughed at the same time and Beech couldn't move or say anything. Then he dreamed that he had been tied down in the hayfield and a huge baler chopped, churned, and ate its way toward him. In the dream he got baled up tightly, and a huge white spider stored him carefully in Summerhill's barn. When he finally left his barn at two-thirty, he felt a ghostly insecurity at not having his shotgun with him. He almost didn't go across the fence, even though the dumb fools were standing close to him, leisurely chewing their cud. But he decided it would be best to go through with it for the sake of making a clean job of letting the cows recover. If Summerhill wasn't aware of it now, he would be if they strolled into the barn, bursting with milk in the morning. One-third would be enough this time—after that he didn't give a damn. There was no sense in carrying the plausibility of the thing too far.

He had to be careful of the bull, if it was still there, so he crept up to the six cows and dumped some of the grain he brought behind them and drove them toward the tree. The wind was running toward Summerhill's house, so the bull would smell the grain first. When they were closer to the tree he saw the bull's dim form blocking out the blackness of the maple; he rested the can and pail near, and it was digging its horns into the bark. Beech began walking inconspicuously toward another tree down the fenceline, hands in pockets, making no noise at all, and the bull saw him, turned and began making a direct line toward his objective at the fence. At first Beech saw it coming slowly, walking without much interest, and he kept his pace, but the bull gained speed, he gained speed, the bull trotted, he ran—and he got there first. It was like making a victory of one of the numerous childhood dreams of running glue-legged from vicious dogs on long chains. He caught his pants on the fence and ripped one pantleg from the knee to the heel. There were dark spots of blood on his leg, where the barbed wire had scratched. When he was over, facing the bull across the fence, he said, "Missed me," softly, and began making his way back toward the maple. He diverted the bull by dropping a handful of grain over the fence. From then on he wasn't bothered by it.

When one-third of the first cow's milk was gone, he started the second and noticed a light from Summerhill's house. He remained perfectly still and watched a shadow cross it, and then the lights went off. He went on milking.

When he was milking the last cow, he heard a small noise in the woods—he couldn't tell what it was, but he finished with frightened haste and crept through the fence stealthily, glad that the wet leaves didn't make any noise. The sound seemed to him either one of an animal wheezing or a human suppressing a laugh, he couldn't tell which. If it was a laugh, it was Summerhill. But he figured that's what he had been looking for, and thinking it was a laugh was just his mind playing tricks on him. Before he left the fence with the milk, he looked around in the woods carefully and could find no trace of an animal or a man. Passing it off, he tied his pantleg around his knee and lugged the milk back to his barn.

After Morgan picked the milk up that morning, Beech went back into the house and fell asleep in the living room chair without eating any breakfast. His mother woke him up at ten and told him Summerhill was waiting in the driveway, and he went out.

"Howdy," Summerhill said from the truck as Beech walked across the lawn.

"Hi," he said, and Summerhill got out of the truck and leaned on the cab. There was a short silence, and Beech could not look straight at him, so he studied something down the hill. "Well," he said slowly, trying to be detached, "How's business?" and Summerhill smiled.
"Good, now," he said. "Miraculous recovery. They're almost up to snuff right now. Ain't that somethin'?"

"Good," Beech said, trying his best to act surprised and interested, but it sounded flat, irreconcilably false. "That's awful good."

"How's yours doin' Nate?" Summerhill asked, and then Beech knew that he had been seen, last night probably, and his ears began to ring. But he stood and maintained as much nonchalance as his nerves would permit and figured slowly, deliberately, saying it to himself as he looked at Summerhill's feet, maybe not, maybe I just got to the place where everything sounds that way.

"Dropped a little," he said.

"Sure is funny," Summerhill said, "how the number of cans you ship and the number I ship always seem to add up the same," and Beech looked at him blankly, his ears ringing again. Then Summerhill smiled at him, smiled as though the both of them should slap their knees and laugh.

"I—I don't know," Beech said, and Summerhill's expression changed, and he slapped his knee slowly and shook his head.

"Okay, you want it private and easy, no screwin' with the law, or do you want to play it rough?" Beech looked at him with wonder, felt his dry voice say:

"What—what do you mean?" Then Summerhill quieted down and got to the business of what Beech wanted at the store. He acted cold, and Beech muttered, "hamburgers 'n eggs," and went back to the house.

And now his mother sat in the hallway, a cup of coffee balanced unsteadily on her knee. "Well?" she asked, cocking her head.

"Well, what?"

"*Well*," she said, but sharply, a way he could only remember her sounding when he had been caught smoking in the barn when he was fourteen, and he tried to hold down his nervousness, but it crept up into his head and made him begin shaking uncontrollably, he hoped unnoticeably, and then, slowly, it began to die.

"Okay," she said, putting her coffee on the half wall between the kitchen and the living room, nodding and sitting up in her wheelchair. "You got anything to tell me?"

"Huh?"

"*Nathan*," she said, "do you have anything . . ."

"What do you mean?" he asked, now becoming more controlled, even adding a bit of agitation to his voice, almost enjoying it. She glared at him.

"Since when do we milk at two in the morning?" she asked, and he screwed his face up as though he didn't understand

her. She lifted her hands up and let them fall on the arms of
her chair. "Stand me up," she said.

"What?"

"Stand me *up*," she repeated, and he stood still and looked
down at her with exaggerated surprise.

"But—but the doctors said . . ."

"The doctors be damned!" she shouted, and then began
struggling in the wheelchair, continuing in a high squeak, "So
help me if this thing slips out from under me—stand me up!"
He did, grabbed her thin arms gently and lifted her to standing, and she reached out for support from the halfwall and
writhed free of his grip. Then she looked at him as he hovered
over her, snorted once and slapped him in the face as hard as
she could. It was little more than a pat. She sat down again.

"There," she said, and he stood gaping at her, his hand on
his face.

"You lunkhead, sneakin' around in the brush at two in the
mornin', milkin' other men's cows—you oughtta be ashamed
of yourself," she said, lowering her voice to a painfully slow
grate.

"But—I—"

"Shame on you," she said. He could not look at her.

"I had to," he said after a long pause.

"Nuts," she said, sitting up in her chair. "And that light
pole—you could get into trouble doin' that stuff." She paused.
"Why?"

"Because, I couldn't let everything just stop. What I mean
is—"

"That's no reason," she said, sighing and looking out of the
window. "Coulda milked 'em by hand," she went on. She
sighed again and there was a short silence. Then she shook
her head, looking up at him.

"What the hell's the use," he muttered. He could not seem to
get it through to her. "I just don't wanna end up workin' for
somebody else and lettin' this place . . ." He stopped,
shrugged, looked at her stern face once more and went into
his bedroom.

He sat down on the bed and put his head down in his hands
and tried to think of what he would say to them. By now
Summerhill had the story around, the Light people were getting ready to take away his power, Morgan would not come up
any more. He looked up—through the window he could see

part of the road that ran up from town, and there was a car on it, coming fast. He jerked his legs as if to get up quickly, then stopped and shrugged again. It was no use. Then the lights went out. He heard his mother wheeling quietly down the hall to her bedroom.

Someone was in the driveway—he supposed it was Summerhill, and he saw the front of a green car. It was a sheriff's car, and he thought, so they got the police. It didn't seem as though he had done anything bad enough for them to get the police. Soon all three of them would be out there, waiting for him. He stood up, grabbed the old shotgun off the wall and looked at it closely, ran his hand along the blued barrels. It has to look like an accident, he thought. Wouldn't want it around that I meant to do it. He went to his desk, opened one of the side drawers and pulled out a shell. Remington, 12, no. 2, it read, and he broke the shotgun and slid the shell in the chamber. Then he got his cleaning kit out from under the bed and opened it. Outside, someone laughed, and a fat man in khaki pointed at the barn, then wrote something in a pad. Beech spread the contents of the cleaning kit out on the bed and put the rod together and placed it on the floor. He paused and looked at the shotgun.

Then he laughed. He could not do it. He tried again, turned it and clicked the hammer back, tightened his jaw and tried hard to look into the barrel—he could not get himself to do it. He felt a faint nausea at having the muzzle that close to his face, and he quickly opened the shotgun and took out the shell, put the shotgun on the bed and rose slowly, his heart thumping fast and his ears ringing.

He felt dizzy, and the nausea remained, as though he had a touch of some kind of fever and was now just getting over it. He laughed again. The living room and kitchen were dark, gray like the moonlight in the pasture where he did his milking. The dizziness and the nausea were going away, and when he opened the door they turned and looked at him. The little man was there, Summerhill, and the sheriff. They all had the looks on their faces. He walked across the lawn, and the sheriff stepped forward first, holding his pad and pencil.

"What's the trouble here?" Beech asked, looking with wonder at them.

Ashes

The sirens that you hear never seem to stop near your door. They are loud and become softer, or they wail softly in the distance and then cease, because it never seems to be your own emergency. It is urgency for strangers. This time, though, it was the opposite. In fact so much so that I got there before the wail did. Ran down the stairs because I heard a vicious contact of metal on metal at great speed, hard to describe because the whunk sound has in it some kind of matter that ripples with ugly energy across your flesh at the time of contact. A shock wave of a sort, fatal to those involved in its source.

A girl I know—knew. But I didn't find out till the next day when a friend of mine came over to tell me that she was dead. "You know Leanne, uh, Leanne . . ."

"Arthur? Leanne Arthur?" I said. "You mean it was her? Leanne Arthur?" A Negro girl, and already, when the name itself was sinking in, something about the thing began to bother me. There was the funny feeling that I was supposed to remember something.

But anyway I ran out there. Five, six people, one woman bent over a girl lying right in the middle of the street. It made me think of a time my brother and I would lie in the middle of the desolate highway on which we lived, lie there on the big dotted line and laugh because there just wasn't ever any chance of a car coming. Do it some time. Examine the paint that erodes away into a relief map, imagine the macadam the bottom of an ocean whose water sloshes eternally against somebody's white cliffs. Then, after being drawn to this, you will swallow, nausea creeping into your chest, because a car might have come in that split second when your imagination robbed your sense of where you were.

A man administered to the guy, and then the driver of the Volks stood helplessly over the girl. Who had evidently gone over the boy's head as he drove his motorcycle right into the space where the front bumper of the Volks separates from the front fender by six inches about like a bicyclerack which may have made me think for a second of those cartoons where accidents are bloodless and decapitations are temporary.

A doctor was now leaning over the girl trying to give her mouth-to-mouth resuscitation. And the girl, and I didn't know who it was because it was just after dusk, the girl was sweating, and there was an expression, sleeping anguish, maybe a bad dream, maybe the look they get with pleasure, but it was expression, and when the doctor moved her she was with expression but limp, her head wanted to stay on the pavement, and her body was like meat. Gravity was pulling her down. She was not resisting gravity. When we are alive we resist gravity. The doctor wanted her to breathe. It was then that the anxious flat metal whine of the siren began, way off, and my legs, rubberized, wanted to help. But there were enough people around, so I stood there trembling.

At my feet, which were on the curb, I saw the trickling of the blood into the gutter. It pooled there, black and shining, with bits of gutter filth floating on it, and there was the funny desire to have them raise her head because, as if by some mysterious upstream journey, the desolate filth could somehow get inside her head and defile it. And the desire to say something was strong. She needed something clean under her head, something white or striped, but not astringent and deliberately dead in a hospital.

The motorcycle guy sat up shaking his head, and the sirens blasted close and police were there too with the red lights that don't turn all the way around. They swung on you again and again with red accusation. Bits of glass glittered on the street and the lady next to me said, "I saw it all . . . the boy just sort of fell and she flew over his head. I saw it. No helmets of course." She sounded righteous and sad, and I couldn't help thinking, "that is not important."

The girl would not wake up. The doctor's face said this to the policeman, who, big and hammy blue above the belt, called on the spurt-spurt radio that droned its numbers into the night.

Still she would not wake up, and the doctor put the stethoscope under her breast (was, is, full, her legs graceful and her face soft and beautiful and always sort of bewildered looking as she shows somebody a picture she has painted about which she says, "Well, I'm sorry, I don't know," because she doesn't and nobody cares anyway). And the doctor's face said to her face that she was not responding properly. They took her in the ambulance. Lifted her gently, and her expression was the same, it had the soft, melancholy anguish on it, as though she had been rudely surprised, almost to the point of physical pain, way inside her head which would not respond. Where was she? What did her brain think? And now, cold—no amount of anything, briny solutions, fish or wonder drugs can help it.

And so the anguished expression stayed with me. After they took her away, the next day when off I went to my classes. Wondering if she was all right, why she had been in the accident, and what her sadness meant. On the way down the street there were the bits of glass and there was the stump of a flare and there in the middle was the spot where her head was, and the broken, sometimes dividing line of brick red, almost brown, on black, coming down into the gutter, and in the gutter the dried black-red pool which now had bugs on it and a cigarette stub with lipstick and I damned the lady who threw it there and hated her for minutes.

All day I wondered who she was, sure that I didn't know her and hoping that she was all right (or as some say, "hoping that she was somebody I knew and disappointed if she turned out to be all right"). No. Admitting that it occurred to me that she might die and I might know her, I still wanted her to live. Even not knowing her I wanted her to live. Because she was sweating and something bothered her. Because when she went over his head and saw the pavement coming, over the wretched fear, she seems to have understood something fundamental and negative, and it shows in the look on her face, the wet, sad and surprised look which gravity will destroy. Know that. Look at a photograph of a man dead two days. His flesh, plagued by weakness in life, runs like ponderous batter off his skull; his features turn toward the ground, which pulls and pulls with unrelenting gentleness.

My room is small, and I live out of a suitcase still, although I have been here for some time. I do not paint, as did Leanne Arthur. I study "Comparative Literature" (those who can't create, compare, they say, pouring the coffee from the saucer into the cup).

And so when I found out, I was in my room, and my girl was there. (This year I have only one, which is enough. Last year, stud that I was, I had two and was pushing for three but sweaty intrigue and guilt stopped that. I drink less, too. My life is a yawing, clumsy journey hopefully toward being good.) My friend came in and said, "You know that girl that was in the accident? She's dead, and you know Leanne, uh, Leanne . . ."

"Arthur? Leanne Arthur? You mean it was her who was in the—it was her who died?" I stood up, already bothered by something.

"Never woke up," he said.

And the talk went on, and all the time, the melancholy look that locked her face bothered me. I couldn't shake it. Later my friend said that she was just going downtown to get some cigarettes, after a party that they had at an apartment uptown.

And then he said how sad it was that she liked this cynical white guy who lived up there, and how she was really young and didn't know if she should stay with him in his place and what would her parents say and so she just painted and apologized for her work which was not bad, and the cynic (and what went on in his mind, stud that he is? I know him. Did he have visions of the soft flesh, of expressions as he, with his lover's gentle and calculated brutality, watches and experiments with stimulus-response, cause-effect?) who liked her, wanted her to live with him and she was in the process of deciding.

"You know the type of guy," my friend said, "he comes out of his place in the morning, and you say 'nice day, isn't it?' and he looks up with all that dejection and tragedy and says, 'I don't think it's so good really.' You know the type." And she was deciding. Apologizing for her paintings and deciding. My friend said that at the party she had really already decided to live with the cynic but didn't know it yet.

Maybe it's because I admired her looks. Maybe for her talent or for her simplicity. Maybe even loved her. I don't know. When it came out that it was her whose face sweated and locked itself in that melancholy release that comes after seeing something fundamental and negative, when it turned out to be her, then I got troubled with the incompleteness of the thing. I thought about it too much. There was something I needed to remember.

Later my girl said, "Why do you keep looking out at the street like that? Did you sleep with her or something?"

"No. No. No. It's just that I'm trying to remember. (I was a little drunk by then.) Say, you know that once she probably saw something nobody else . . . picked up a Lincoln-head penny and saw a spider on a fireplug? No. Walked up a street and thought 'so and so's coming around that corner right now' and bap! So and so? I mean she—she . . . " I laughed then, because it just couldn't be explained. There was the thing that I was trying to remember even when I was drunk. I saw her very little, spoke to her not at all except maybe a single word or two a couple times. Something I saw her do.

Still tried, on the way to school, and I stopped by the dried pool. Not red any more, just a blackish stain, and the cigarette stub was brown, the broken line from the middle of the street almost gone. I thought, she herself is cold (maybe not in the center, maybe it takes a lot of time; maybe she will get up and walk away).

When I was young I looked at the corpse of a dog and I speculated on the way its body hugged the ground. The details of animals dead by the road, hairless baby birds under trees. Pictures in magazines. When I cut myself I always smelled and tasted the blood.

There was something that I couldn't remember. I wanted to. If it came back, then I would have a chance at understanding at least some of the expression. My room is small and I live out of a suitcase although I have been here for some time. Those who can't create, compare. Maybe it's in the paintings that she did. Abstract, colorful. No, nothing there. But I wish I could own one. Maybe in her knowing the cynic who wanted her. He has something important to do with it.

Maybe only in my room. Maybe it is one of those things where it takes something of yours and something of someone else's to add up to whatever you need. In my room there are books, an easy chair and a bed (on which my girl sits, sewing my socks with her spectacles perched on her nose, looking more like my grandmother than the girl I have with me on weekends). On the floor there is dust, gray cigarette ashes. There is my suitcase.

Three days after she died, it rained and I looked out the window at the street where the cigarette stub lay in the stain of her blood and I realized that all of that would be gone and so with it the last of her evidence. We could shrug and continue on.

Somewhere in that same day I remembered what it was that completed the thing and made it crystallize in my mind. Once

I saw her at a party, self-conscious and living inside her head. Then something funny happened and she laughed, that's all. Somehow she broke loose and laughed hard, her face silhouetted against the window, real laughter that was too much payment to whatever was supposed to be funny. The laughter took off on its own somehow, idiotic and defiant, and coaxed her so that she went ahead with it, other people laughing too, and it was laughter that said look at me because I am young and I am never going to die. Look at my face, smooth, with full lips, at my hands that make things. Hear the husky sandiness of my voice that is only nineteen or twenty-four, watch me walk without thought of the ground. Laughter that said, I am deciding. I will always, always be able to decide. Look at me, because no matter what happens, I am never going to die.

Idiot's Rebellion

When my father saw Mike outside looking sadly and gesturing vaguely over the patch of raw dirt where our old dog was
just buried, he said, "Look at the big goon—blubberin' over a
dog! Jaysus!"

But the rest of us were surprised and curious—feelings of
grief were supposed to be above him. Mike was retarded, and
up till then we assumed that his brain was as blank as the
inside of a football as far as normal, complex human thoughts
were concerned. There was something about his birth. My
mother was too young, or some mysterious circumstance in
his fetal growth left incomplete what I remember thinking of
as the complex circuitry of the underside of a TV set, but in
miniscule form. Where nerve cells joined and were supposed
to zap each other a million times a second in a kind of complex
and dazzling harmony, he had little burned out resistors, tiny
dead bulbs, shorted wires and misdirected currents, so that
the TV set of his brain yielded only a snowy and warped
pattern in undulating vertical movement, with a toneless hum
for a background. We knew his hearing wasn't good, and the
best my mother could do in the earlier years of attempts to
cure him with the marginal services of the backcountry was to
have him labeled marginally autistic, but trainable.

My father stomped out to him and began shoving him
toward the tractor and wagon, gradually distracting him from
his feelings. The field out back was tightly crisscrossed by
dotted lines of amber bales of hay, and Mike, who was more
pack animal than human to my father, would pick them up
and hurl them over the sideracks of the wagon to my older
brother Paul and me. The ninety-pound oblong blocks, trailing golden chaff, would clear the six-foot sideracks by two feet.
With his hands flat on Mike's back, my father trudged him
toward his work while he dully approached comprehension
of what was next. And when he slowed up, balked like a mule,
my father took his hat off and whipped it repeatedly against
the back of Mike's head. Paul said "prick" under his breath.

We used that word because *bastard* or *son of a bitch* would
have been compliments. Paul and I hated my father with an
intense passion and regarded our own lives, brutalized daily

by filthy, back-breaking work, as a continuous, subtle revolution against his tyranny. The symbol of our revolution was Mike, six-feet-three and well over two hundred pounds and as strong and indestructible as a cross between a bull and a gorilla. It seems to me that he spent most of his time in the gutters shoveling fresh manure into the spreader. His characteristic expression was one of the serene objectivity of a world-weary genius. At times he could manifest a kind of dull happiness, which showed itself in a slight modification of his facial expression. He made almost no sounds except grunts or yells of pain when he was beaten by my father.

Mike could take care of himself on a minimal basis where normal hygiene was concerned, and ate with a tablespoon alone before the rest of the family sat down. I remember that Paul and I as little children made a daily ritual out of watching him — he would lift a gob of potato salad the size of a tennis ball on that spoon, and with a mystifying lack of effort, consume it all in a long, thoughtful swallow. Then he would chase it with a glass of milk taken in a single omnivorous gulp. He was so strong that for us he was a kind of hero, now the symbol of suffering caused by my father, earlier a trusty riding animal, our King Kong or carnival strong man, capable of feats of strength of comic-book heroes — lifting the front end of the big Farmall off the ground, carrying four bags of feed at once, bending metal rods in his hands.

My father beat him frequently, once every two or three days with belts, pieces of wood, tools, and his only response was a toneless yell at the pain only, as if his anger were directed at some vague cause from the sky and the figure before him flailing away with the belt either could not be connected with the pain or was too sure a standard in his life to question.

Sometimes these beatings were for good reason, we knew, to break him of what my mother called his "phases" of pointless or destructive activity. Deep in my memory is the picture of Mike at fifteen, caught by my father and brother and I in the act of invading what was supposed to be our bull's territory. What angered my father most, when he saw the boy looking dully in his direction, seemingly unaware of the position he was in with his jeans down over his boots and the cow's tail up in his fist, was that he selected for his partner a valuable, dewey-eyed Jersey rather than one of the highboned Holsteins. Another time Mike developed a fascination for fire, so that for a long time before I was ten I never really slept well because of fearful dreams of going up in smoke in the night. We caught him, always in the nick of time it seemed, setting obscure corners of the barn or house on fire—he always had those whitened patches of burned skin on his fingertips from frequent accidents with the matches. I remember feeling that my father's violent curing of this behavior was harsh but just.

Sometimes Paul and I wanted to beat him for interfering in our lives. Once, on a hot summer day that would end at a drive-in theater, a rare and important occasion, we made the mistake of taking him with us for a quick swim down at the bridge. Once he got in the water we could not get him out, and as dusk advanced and Paul and I screamed at him and tried to tow him out, struggling for purchase in the neck-deep water, we saw our chances to get to the movie evaporate because of the goddamned stupid mule soaking comfortably on into the evening.

But that night, after we saw him show emotion over the dead dog, Paul and I were awake in our room, talking about what it meant. "There's goddamn sure somethin' goin' *on* in there!" he said. I was thirteen, Paul fifteen—both of us had always been sure that something important was locked inside our older brother and expected someday for it to emerge. My heart was high in my chest at the thought that at twenty, Mike was now gaining an intelligence. Maybe tomorrow he would even say something.

We were sure that, being denied the intelligence of a normal human, he was therefore in possession of a potent intuitive sense—if we had dropped him by parachute in say Portland, Oregon, he would lumber with unerring accuracy across the continent back home to us, his perfect sonar equipment directing him in as sure a sixth sense as those legendary dogs who proved their superiority to humans in the same way, Balto of the North or Gray Dawn. Those same dogs lacked something obvious in their reasoning capacity, we knew. They could find their way home across thousands of miles of rough territory, but once tethered up, they would spend the rest of their lives running hopefully at some imaginery freedom only to be jerked brutally at the end of the chain, and they would do it over and over again.

But a number of things happened around that time, more than ten years ago it is now, which put our adolescent convictions about Mike to the test.

There was in our family one growing light—our little sister Stephanie, who was three the time we all saw Mike grieve over the dog and nearly six the winter she died. Where Mike had been denied intelligence by the shaky hand of whatever created him, Stephanie made up for it with a brilliance that awed all of us. A lot of this had to do with the benefits of television, which gave her an alien sophistication in her speech. At three when she was surprised by something she could say, "Isn't that simply amazing!" or "how remarkable!" She lived away from the diseased core of the family, my father and his sons who hated him for his brutality, and she was spared ever having to see Mike, her favorite, being beaten. It always happened in the woods or in the barn where Mike would err in his simple tasks and the inevitable would happen, so that Paul and I would stand off grinding our teeth while the flailing would be carried out against the uncomprehending victim, with the tractor running at half-throttle in the driveway to drown out the yells. Three minutes later, still grinding our teeth and muttering "prick!" under our breaths, we would hear my mother report some new gem of the child's genius. "She said, 'my goodness, the tractor was so loud I almost got a cold!' " to which my father would say, "Aww, ain't that the cutest goddamn thing you ever heard?"

The times my father was off on some business in town were for Mike sunny, utopian days where Stephanie would lead him off on various excursions around the buildings—nature walks where she would lecture to him with formal haughtiness about the interesting facts of natural history, or they would play, she serving him imaginary cups of tea with toy utensils which were absurdly tiny in his massive, battered hands. He bore for her a solid, total devotion, harmless as far as we were concerned. But sometimes we wondered, too, when we saw him standing there, huge and muscular, with that large bulge of denim at his crotch, and remember the simple fact of his mental condition and combine that with fears of unexpectedly irrational behavior, like that time with the little Jersey. Seeing them going off to the woods farther and farther away each time, Stephanie chattering to him with her air of motherly superiority, and him hulking down so that she could hold his little finger, would bring about that flash of the whole question of sex and the tiny, unsuspecting girl. Paul wasn't that worried, but for a while I was nearly obsessed about it, and thought it incredible and ridiculous that no one else seemed concerned enough to do anything about it.

Finally Stephanie said something bright and naive at the

dinner table, and my father coughed on his food and my mother tried to mediate in her haggard way. Apparently while they were in the woods Mike had to heed the call of nature and simply lumbered to a halt and flopped out that mammoth sausage which Paul and I agreed years later could easily be called "mythical." Their outings were stopped—it was best, my mother said, that we shouldn't let them get too close. After all, Stephanie would be getting to know other pretty little girls her age soon, and so playing with a grown boy didn't seem to her appropriate at all. Did it to us? We shuffled around and said, gee, well, I guess not. Whatever.

Stephanie balked, as did Mike. Whenever she was advised to stay away from him she would sulk and stomp off to her room, and Mike, as if he sensed the ghost of his former playmate present, wandered, a little stooped, off to the woods. That was all right, except that after a couple of weeks he was gone three hours, then all morning, then on into the afternoon. Mike could not connect the harsher treatment given him by my father with his absence from his fate, fresh manure, bales of hay, rocks. Paul and I developed this vision of him going to the woods simply to kind of commune with nature, with silence itself. Maybe he even got to know animals, like that kid Mowgli of the Jungle. We assumed that there was some mysterious but important purpose he followed. At this time I was fourteen, Paul sixteen. Later our speculations would become more realistic.

But it happened again and again. He would return and my father would start the tractor and grab a milking machine strap and give him five or ten shots across the back, yelling, "Ya goddamn goon! Don't you ever learn nothin'?"

And after we would try to explain to him that he was staying away too long, and that was why he now felt the welts from the strap. But Mike only turned his head and stared gravely into the wind, toward the trees in the distance beyond the back hayfield. Paul might continue explaining, and Mike would walk off into the barn and pick up the manure shovel and slop the stuff into the spreader, gazing in what appeared to be a thoughtful manner at his work.

As a response to the general confusion caused by his new situation, he had a relapse back to his fire obsession. One day Paul and I were walking out of the barn and saw Paul's red Fokker Triplane, a valuable relic from our model plane days, soar from the attic window trailing smoke. I broke into a run toward the house as it did its graceful spiral toward the ground, and then saw my blue Vought Corsair with its sleek, lowered wings angling down toward the road on fire. After taking a quick look at the black skeletons of smoking balsa wood, we ran up to the attic and found him preparing our lesser achievements for their last dive. His face ashen with rage, Paul snatched the matches from Mike and bulled him toward the attic door, cursing violently at the back of his head. It was, we decided, Mike's re-creation of what all of us had seen so often on "Victory at Sea."

Gradually our speculations about Mike and his secret life changed. By fall of that year Paul and I both gained a digit in our ages. We'd be cleaning milking machines:

"Yeah, that's it," Paul would say, scratching the pail with the Brillo, "he's beatin' off, that's what it is."

"Three hours?"

"Hell, it's a big job." We both snickered.

"Yeah, suppose the ground rumbles?"

"Yeah, animals run away. Trees wilt."

I stopped. At the time it came to me that sexual desire was a strange question where Mike was concerned. "Do you think he still gets feelin's in that direction?"

"Sure, he's human ain't he?"

"Yeah. Dogs do too, even though they can't think."

"An' you know how he likes to go off by himself, even when he wants to take a dump. I guess that's why he's off now. He's *secret.*"

But it still seemed to me too questionable a feature for Mike's character, that women and desire were for a much more complex mind, one that was capable of reasoning out the sin of it and connecting it to an attitude you could call worldly. The Jersey cow was only a freak of circumstance and long forgotten by now. It was out of Mike's league, and therefore I didn't believe Paul's speculation. I preferred the Mowgli theory, and this theory was sustained by the fact that Mike could disappear in a way that made following him impossible. He traveled too fast, with that crafty intelligence lower animals have that we humans have forgotten in the long road of evolution, that sixth sense we traded in for reason. There was a nest of black bears out there that he socialized with, or maybe it was the deer—he would climb the crabapple trees and feed them in return for their friendship.

Another thing that affected this attitude was that around this time my father suddenly figured it was manly to brag to his sons about his exploits, probably assuming that it was an acceptable way to teach sex to us. The result was kind of ludicrous—we would sit bouncing along in the truck and frequently screw our faces up at each other whenever he carried on about it, playing the steering wheel around the potholes.

"I counted 'em, boys ... hardly a woman around I ain't plowed one time or another."

We'd pass neighbors' farms, each a quarter mile or so apart. "Harrison's ... there's a nice filly in there one of you oughtta try to sport." Then at the bend below the hill on which our farm sat: "Smith's ... one time me and that missus did it in the water down to the bridge." Paul would cough, and in his breath I could hear the word "bullshit," because we liked Mrs. Smith and felt that it would have shown her to have no taste at all to have done that with my father. "There's the stamp collector's," he said, "he's got a mysterious sorta spinster daughter ... like to plank that one some time." The stamp collector was an old man we all knew had a large and, we figured, priceless stamp collection. As for his daughter, we had never seen her up close. "Now let me tell you about this here roofer guy's wife, some little things you should know about how skirts behave ...." Bullshit too, because she was just too young.

And on it would go. At the Post Office he would go in to do business and Paul would say something like, "if he says one more word about this I'm gonna puke right on the goddamn dash! My lunch is in my goddamn throat!"

The fact was that Mike had to be as different as possible from my father, aloof and lonely in his suffering. For him, desire of that confusing sort was out of character and too demeaning of his austerity.

Then a lot changed in a short time. I was sixteen and Paul was heading for graduation and the service, a future that made him turn distant and kind of philosophical about life. He and I both had girls. We both saw the end of the tunnel, were both old enough that we began seeing Mike as a sad case, an idea that was being left behind. Both our girls were the looser types who didn't associate with town girls and Paul and I, moving quickly into the complexities of adulthood, developed a greater sense of the magnitude of Mike's hopeless deprivation. Paul and I both carried with pride the symbol of our graduation, inside secret compartments in our wallets, so that the outside surface would have that telltale ring of raised leather made by the condoms inside. And Mike, endlessly slopping manure into the spreader—what it all came down to with him was that beating off in the woods was all he would ever get.

In late winter, after most of the snow had melted, Stephanie went off on an excursion into the woods and disappeared into a freak snowstorm. I remember this as a blur of dogged activity, of tromping through the waist-deep snow from sunup to sundown, for three days, while above sometimes we heard the helicopters of the state troopers flopping in the sky with a deafening clatter. Neighbors from all over helped, would come out of the woods exhausted at sunset, breath vapor curling away from their faces, and gesture from a hundred yards with sustained shrugs. All through this experience I cultivated a hope I knew was irrational and a product of my childhood, that Mike's special abilities would produce a miracle of some kind. He helped in the woods too, and I waited throughout all of it for him to come through. I also saw the degree of my father's humanity emerge—he was destroyed by the loss, worse off than my mother, who seemed the most stoic of all of us. She had taken by then to reading the Bible and watching Sunday morning church programs, and singing when the people did on TV.

Mike's sonar did pay off, but two weeks too late, after we had accepted the loss of the only unsullied purity our family possessed. One day after the snow had again melted, we were outside collecting up stovewood lost under the receding winter snow and heard a kind of animal roar, a combination of a call for help and a scream of rage. Then Mike broke into view out of the woods in a hunched sprint, sending explosions of snow off his feet, carrying something. He must have assumed that the little sitting statue he found could be brought back to life if he only rushed her back to the warmth of the house. When he arrived and placed her gently at our feet, he then turned and screamed again, gesturing with both hands at the woods. My father went into glassy-eyed shock and my mother would not come out of the house. Paul held Mike by the shoulders, talking to him, calming him down. As if in a dream I leaned down, stunned and airy, and touched her face, I guess to clean the bits of snow from her eyes and mouth. Her cheek was soft, but only a quarter of an inch in, where the still frozen flesh stopped my finger.

Where my father seemed most human during the horror of

Stephanie's death and funeral, he swung the other way after it, partly because of an embarrassment caused by Mike at the end of the funeral. My mother insisted that he come, that all the children of God receive the privileges of the last parting. Whenever she talked this way Paul and I would flush with embarrassment at this new feature of her behavior. My father grunted suspiciously that it was okay, but only if he stayed in the truck. He hated anyone seeing his retarded son and was always afraid of being made a fool of by him, and my mother's new religion was a problem for him since all God's creatures were supposed to receive the same privileges. He wasn't sure he liked that.

At the end of the funeral after we all stood around watching the little casket being lowered into the ground, we returned to our vehicles with the sound of shoveling behind us, each of us alone with the awful sadness at the fact of leaving Stephanie in the ground. We were already climbing into the truck and car when we discovered that Mike wasn't there.

We had to search around the church for five minutes. Paul and my father found him behind the church in the graveyard surrounded by a few neighbors who tried to reason with Mike that Stephanie was dead and there was no use in his trying to dig her up like that. He was down in the partly filled hole, muddy and digging with his hands, while the two volunteer churchmen stood above with their shovels discussing whether or not it would be safe to try to stop him. We had just missed the neighbor who went to the car to tell us of Mike's appearance. My father was pale and nearly without expression as he explained that poor Mike was not himself. Paul pulled him out of the hole and convinced him to return to the truck. And Mike—the expression on his face was the same as always, except that now you could see in his eyes a kind of irrational look of desperate optimism. He was sure she was still alive.

My father allowed himself one day of silent grief before he returned with a vengeance to his old self. On some excuse, in the barn, he laid a milking machine strap with a whack across Mike's shoulders, and then went kind of berserk. I remember mostly the shadows, because when he dropped the strap and picked up the two-by-four, I stumbled around a corner and Paul went to them, saying, "Pa! Don't! You'll ..."

"You stay the hell outta this!" he roared. Neither of us was prepared for any physical confrontation with him. He was too big and now, too insane. Against the whitewashed wall in the dim light of the single forty-watt bulb on the ceiling, I saw the hulking shadow of Mike protecting his face and head with his forearms while my father beat with the two-by-four from above and the sides, screaming, "Goddamned worthless goon! Don't you understand nothin'? Ain't you got no goddamn sense?" and Mike yelled with each shot in a loud, pleading whimper that made me hunker down and cover my face with my hands and Paul, tough Paul, now seemingly in such complete possession of himself, beat the manger wall with his fists and sobbed hoarsely, "I hate this! Goddamn I hate this, I hate this!" When my father dropped the board and stumbled out we went and found Mike standing there bleeding, and sort of sadly dumbfounded. His face was streaked with tears, his forehead was cut and welted and his forearms were covered with large, open lacerations.

Standing on rubbery legs, Paul and I washed out the wounds in the milk house, speculating in quavering voices on whether or not any bones were broken. We both realized at that moment that Mike, all our lives the symbol of indestructibility, like a mountain or a mythical animal, was as vulnerable and mortal as anyone, and his future, all futures, seemed somehow bleak and hopeless and brutal. I had never seen Paul so shaken—he kept looking into Mike's eyes, trying to reason it all out, it seemed. Then he swallowed and said, "The prick is gonna kill you." He said it softly because he was having trouble controlling his voice. "He's gonna kill you because he hates you." Then he spun around, stomped and gestured angrily at the wall. "Jesus Christ!" he shouted.

"I'll go get some bandages," I said. My voice was high and hollow, kind of flat like the sound of an old radio in another room. "Bandages, that's what I'll get."

Paul looked at me, still glassy-eyed, "You understand that don't you, even if he doesn't. I'm outta here in three months. You in another year or two."

"I'm stayin'. I'll watch 'im."

"No you won't. You can't." Then he turned to Mike again, put his hands on his shoulders and said, "You got to fight back." I knew what he was up to. As boys we had often considered training him to swing back for every time he was swung on. We realized that this made him the winner, hands down. The one thing we didn't know was whether or not this was possible— to turn an infinitely serene being into a fighter. It was playing with nature and since my father was the only adversary he would ever need his training for, we knew it was too dangerous.

Paul finally sighed in exasperation and said, "You wouldn't hurt a fly, would you? No, you wouldn't." He paused, thinking, and then said kind of vaguely, " 'At it, you just a big old goon, like he says?"

"Hey," I said, zeroing my eyes in on him and tightening my jaw. It was an old habit, that of being prepared at any moment for the defense of Mike's honor, something Paul and I both did at school. Paul snorted and shook his head.

"Go ahead, swing, I don't give a shit." Then he waved his hand at me and left.

I decided that I would do something radical, I guess because of the weird extremity of the situation. I gestured to Mike to follow me, and took him to the kitchen, where my mother was working at the sink. "Ma, look what Pa done."

She turned, looked, turned back. "Disciplining grown boys is the man's business," she said. Paul watched from the hall. He mouthed the words *fuck you* and held up his middle finger at her back.

"He's hurt real bad," I said. Paul came in and looked at her.

"He's hurt Ma," he said. "Goddammit, he's gonna kill him!"

"Don't you use language like that in this house. Ever."

"You hate him too, don't you?" Paul said. "Either that or you got no guts at all. Or is it the Lord's will? Huh?"

She turned quickly and glared at us, and then spoke with a level, even voice. "Clean up the cuts and bandage them. I have had enough suffering for all my life in the last three weeks."

"You don't deny it then," Paul said. "Boy I'm glad I'm gettin' away from this place." We took Mike up to the bathroom and worked on his wounds.

Paul and I watched him closely as he healed, which took three weeks. He had trouble with his left hand, which probably had been fractured, and with his knee, which was badly bruised. He tried once to go to the woods, but got only fifty yards before he had to turn and hop back home on one foot. He would sometimes stop and look toward the trees, and we figured that the dim memory of Stephanie was what caught his attention, like a mother dog searching for pups after they've been taken away. He was around all the time and the atmosphere was bleak and sad, especially for Paul, who probably felt like a deserter. He no longer talked about what fun it was going to be to travel, about the educational programs they had in the navy, about freedom. He was not going to be free, that was sure, and if I looked into my own future I saw no freedom either.

The truth of it was that Mike would be helpless and it was our responsibility to do something about it. We discussed elaborate plans for taking him with us, for releasing him from what we saw as the horrible remainder of his life, endless work and endless suffering. Paul said he'd be dead in five years at this rate. Without us around he'd only have to work more. But we also exhausted these speculations and settled into feelings of permanent shame—neither of us wanted to admit the obvious: we would escape, physically at least, and Mike would be left to complete his life as my father wished.

For the most part this ends on a sunny Saturday in early spring, one of those days when the countryside oozes with a balmy moisture and the ground is mushy under your feet. It was four weeks after the beating. Things had settled a little—my father had laid off because Mike had to repair before he could take another beating. We heard a car in the driveway and went out, except for my mother and Mike, who was trained not to be seen on those rare times when people came to our door.

It was a woman, and I recognized her as the stamp collector's daughter. She was older than I had thought, but not bad looking. My father stood there with a funny look on his face— she was one he said many times that he surely would like to plow, plank, whose butter he'd like to churn. Now his expression seemed to show it. She stood there in the dirt driveway and her expression changed. She seemed to gradually realize that whatever she was at was a bad idea. We always looked a little scruffy and low class. But she spoke anyway.

"I have some sort of . . . simple work that needs doing, and I need someone to help. My father's not . . . he's kind of old and . . . . Anyway we pay one dollar an hour, but whoever does it has . . . should be . . . strong. I mean . . . *very* strong."

She looked at us with a kind of flush-faced smile.

"Well," my father said jovially, and stepped forward. "No reason why we can't oblige . . . ."

Mike came lumbering around the corner of the house. He saw her and stopped dead in his tracks and looked at the ground, and then again at her, and his face drooped, his eyes became misty with warmth. She shook her head quickly at him, waved him away with short jerks of her hand. Finally she was overcome by her own embarrassment and jumped into her car and spun off, flicking bits of mud back at us.

It was Paul who got it first. He jumped up and down once and said, "Hey!" and then stared after the car, thinking. "Hey, wait a minute!" he said.

"What?" my father said. "What! What!"

Then Paul ran to Mike and dragged him by the arm toward the barn, leaving my father and me staring into space, wondering what had just happened. I ran up to the barn. Paul was screaming with nearly soundless laughter, trying to keep my father from hearing. I had to laugh too, although I didn't know what was so funny.

When that flash of understanding hit it was like one of those cosmic, time-lapse sunrises in the movies. "Mike!" I whispered, "no."

"Yes," Paul said. "Yes! Goddamn! Mike!" He jumped up and punched him on the shoulder.

Through the barn door we could still see my father over by the driveway, staring at the ground and scratching his head. Paul went out of control again. "I'm dyin'!" he yelled. "I'm fuckin' dyin'!" Then he stopped, wide-eyed and curious. "She don't look like no big woman to me. Je-heesus, can you imagine?"

"How long's this been goin' on?"

"Years," Paul whispered in amazement. "Years. Don't you see, this is the first long stretch he ain't been goin' over there, 'cept for blizzards." We figured out that somewhere back there, maybe when Stephanie was two or three and Mike began his mysterious disappearances into the woods, some unlikely series of events occurred where he met the stamp collector's daughter. She got bored while her father was ogling his Hitler heads or something and went for a walk in the woods. While we talked, we saw him move toward the door, his memory again kindled, so that he was looking gravely into the wind with that contemplative and thoughtful expression which was so familiar to us. He'd make a beeline for the far corner of the hayfield that bordered on state reforestation land—only a quarter of a mile beyond that he'd come out above the curve in the road where the stamp collector lived.

We could tell he was going to do this now. "See there?" Paul whispered. "It's something he does normally, like shovelin' shit. Two years at least. Hey," he said, "think of that. She couldn't take it any more, hadda come up after the old stud here." He patted Mike on the shoulder. "Steady big fella," he said. Then he pushed gently. "Go ahead, she's home by now. It's the Lord's will," and he snickered.

"Yeah, can't fight the ol' Lord's will, can you."

Mike turned and looked at us. It could be that there was no expression on his face, but years later when Paul and I talked about this, we were convinced that there was at least the shadow of understanding, that we were his brothers and we approved, and he could have been registering a kind of simple thanks for our support. "Go to it big fella," Paul said.

So he went, limping a little. There was one obstacle left, my father, who now must have understood the meaning of that exchange of facial expressions in the driveway. Mike wasn't going anywhere to humiliate him any more, that was sure. He appeared walking in a straight line, intending a kind of right-angle interception of Mike's progress, his hand already hooked in his belt. I said, "Oh God, here we go again." But the fiery expression Paul had with the recognition of what had been going on now changed into a look of scathing hatred. It must have been that Mike was now worth saving.

"Oh no," he said. "Christ, I'm gone in *two months*, who the hell cares now!" and he ran around in search of a weapon. A pitchfork, since it was close at hand. "Why didn' I think of this before?" he yelled.

"Paul! Hey, c'mon, this is . . . "

"You watch me, man," he said.

He ran out along Mike's path just as my father interrupted Mike, his face twisted with a combination of expressions: anger, wounded vanity, jealousy, and a kind of anxious lust to get at what he seemed to enjoy most, punishing my brother. But Paul got to my father first. Sensing danger, Mike stopped. My father looked at Paul with a kind of condescending questioning on his face.

"Stay the hell outta this," he snapped, whipping out the belt and going for Mike. I saw what I saw next in the bright, impossible light of a dream. In a simple move Paul gripped the fork in two hands like a rail across his chest, and knocked my father down by ramming the handle against his forehead.

I stumbled toward them, giggling with fright and amazement. My father was stunned, struggling to get up, saying, "All right now, all right. What's your trouble?"

"Can't stand it can you?" Paul said. "Big goon here got there first."

"All right. All right now."

"C'mon, get up and hit him with the belt, prick."

"All right."

"Pa? If you ever lay a finger on my brother again, any time, next year or ever, I'll hunt you down and I'll kill you."

"All right."

"Think I'm kiddin', prick? Huh? Think I'm kiddin'?"

"All right."

"Once. You touch him once and I swear I'll find you and I'll kill you."

"All right."

"Now you watch, stud. Watch this." Then he turned to Mike and put his hand on his shoulder. I suddenly felt a funny sense that everything was all very diplomatic now. My father was looking up, a little dazed still, as Paul nudged a little and said, "Go, Mike, go ahead."

And Mike lumbered off toward the corner of the field while we watched.

I suspected some awful confrontation between Paul and my father later that day, but it never happened. My father said to me, vaguely, fingering the lump on his forehead, "That Paul—well, 'f he's goin' to the service, I guess he's gotta be ready to take a fella on." He paused, thinking. "And don't tell your mother about this, about any of it. If Mike's gonna go get his, then . . . Just don't you let your mother ever find out." That was all he said about it. He seemed to be still a little surprised about it all, and there was even a tinge of respect in his voice for Paul, and maybe even for Mike.

Later that day Paul and I found ourselves sitting and watching Mike eat, as we did when we were children. Paul had in his lap a Department of Agriculture topographical map of our area, and showed me how, if you laid a ruler on our house, a tiny square dot, and ran it to the corner of the hayfield before the woods, you'd find that a few inches up on the map the edge of the ruler just whispered past the dot indicating the stamp collector's house. "This is incredible!" Paul whispered. "Straight as a goddamn chalkline!" With his tablespoon, Mike raised huge gobs of stew to his mouth, seemingly listening.

Paul looked up and shook his head. "It's his sonar," he whispered. Then something caught Paul's eye and he leaned forward and picked a long strand of dark hair off Mike's shirt. "Ah ha," he said, holding it up to the light, "elementary, Watson. Why didn't we see this before?" Mike saw the hair and paused, his mouth full of stew, and then his eyes did that slight misty drooping. "Yeah, old Mike," Paul said. "One stud she'll never forget, huh big fella?"

"How does he call her? I mean tell her he's around?"

Paul laughed. "He just pulls a tree out of the ground and waves it around like a flag."

To my knowledge my father never beat Mike again. Paul and I went out into the world, he to the navy and a couple of years later me to the state university. My father later had a stroke and had to sell the place, and the result was that Mike had to be sent to a state home north in the county. By the time this happened there was little Paul or I could do about it.

I did see Mike once again, about seven years after I left home. It was a promise I made to Paul after he got back from the navy. He was going to New York City and didn't have enough time, so I told him I'd go up there and check on Mike. When we talked about him, Paul again got that look on his face, thinking about the stamp collector's daughter. It was just the idea that the one out of the three of us who started out with the most strikes against him got there first anyway, even managed to remain a kind of hero through it all.

When I went to the state home to see him, an attendant smiled and said, "Oh Mike, sure, go right out back—can't miss him." He was walking around the grounds with an ancient lady half his size, and she held his huge hand. When I got close and met his eyes nothing happened. Either he had forgotten or didn't recognize me in the alien clothes. But it didn't matter. He was being well fed, didn't have to bust his ass working, would never again be beaten. And when I walked away I was thinking that if he remembered anything, it would be best to remember the stamp collector's daughter, or maybe those days when he walked out across the bright fields with the tiny girl leading him along, chattering up at him. And about the stamp collector's daughter, I still hold to the secret expectation that some day he will flinch and stop, staring into the wind, and some dormant tube will flash with orange light and some little resistor will connect up, and he'll turn his body in a certain instinctive direction and begin walking south toward her place, climbing fences and angling by roads and towns and swimming rivers in a line as dead perfect as the edge of a ruler.

The Gravity of the Situation

When the special Board of Education committee to judge on the case of Billy Cavanaugh, a sophomore at Warner Central School, recognized that the face of the girl in his pictures belonged to Virginia Jensen, Billy's father beat him for the fifth time since the whole thing started. "Profaning a nice girl like that!" he roared, the cords on his sunburned neck sticking out and vibrating, "Daughter of one of my best friends! Degenerate!"

Finally he stomped off to the kitchen, where Billy's mother fretted softly, "Don't hit him so hard Jim! Please, now, the boy's apologized a hundred times!"

"Jesus H. God, what went wrong?" his father wailed. He held himself in a sustained shrug, looking down at her, the faded cross of the straps of his coveralls marking the slight hump of his back. Then, in a harsh undertone he said, "I told 'im all the things a fella's supposed to tell his son—I'd expect 'im to take 'er out rather 'n draw dirty pictures of 'er."

" 'S not her face," Billy muttered, rubbing his shoulder. He wondered how in hell they ever recognized her. When he drew the pictures he knew the face was hers and did all he could to make it belong to someone else, even made it ugly. Still they saw her face. He went into his room and sat down on his bed, and looking at the black mirror of his window, he thought of going to school tomorrow. The big guys, the seniors and juniors, Monk Perkins and all the other guys, they rooted for him in this thing, probably because they were afraid that Billy'd tell everybody that they had offered money for his dirty pictures.

He opened his window and felt air on the back of his neck. "Ahh." He got his cigarettes out from under the matress and lit one and held it out of the window so that the smoke curled away into the night. A creak in the hall floor would give him his cue to douse the cigarette. Shivering with a kind of giddy, rubber-legged mischief, the same feeling he had when he drew his pictures, he chuckled with black pleasure. But it did not outweigh the seemingly permanent lump of miserable, nauseating shame that he had become used to. It was simply the worst embarrassment of all: his inside life, the dirty activity of his mind had been discovered on paper.

"Pornography," he said softly. Funny word. Seemed like it must have something to do with mathematics. He had never heard it until last week, when he heard his father talking to his mother about how they were going to keep these pornography trials out of the papers. Billy could see it: his father's characteristic after-work pose—sitting hunched over his coffee talking into its vapor, his hand, with bits of grain dust clinging to the black hair, wrapped around the mug. And his mother, rattling away at the sink, always with her head half-turned to listen to him. " —It'll play hell with the store," he said. Billy's father was half owner of the grain store in town. His friend Mr. Jensen was a farmer, and Billy sensed the simple connection. What he did even had financial effects.

Then Billy had this dream every night, where his mother and father and Uncle Fred and people from school all sat around an egg, on which was written a sort of Greek word. Then they were all Indians or prehistoric men, sitting with little or no clothes on around a campfire, all keeping a brooding vigil on the egg. In one dream a little tiny man with a striped suit and spats and a cane and straw derby hat broke the shell and strutted out like a drum major and said all sorts of idiotic things with a sharp nasal twang in his voice. "This is the *storyofadirtyboy*—" Sometimes he'd point his cane at Billy, or at all of them and say, "Nnn*guilty!*" and laugh and strut around the broken shell of his egg.

The face—that was the thing that carried the shame to the third power. He used her face because he liked her, even loved her as a matter of fact. Well, that was over now. He chuckled, blowing smoke into the night. Over? He hardly ever spoke to her. He usually rode to school in the back seat of the bus, and between him and Virginia Jensen would be his friend Richie Jester, who was a friend of hers. So when he spoke to her it was past him, sort of second hand.

The hall floor creaked. Billy flipped the cigarette away, shut the window and wheezed any surplus smoke from his lungs. His father looked in. "What's 'at Counselor fella's name?"

"Uh, Forester?" His father nodded, paused as if he were thinking, and went back to the kitchen. This sudden civility surprised Billy. Prob'ly cause there isn't anything left that could be worse, he thought, smiling with a funny, evil satisfaction. He almost looked forward to tomorrow.

Monk Perkins was the one responsible for his beginning the pictures and his being caught. Monk was a friend of Billy's, but not the type that Richie Jester was. Richie was a good friend and Monk was a bad friend, the type that Billy and Richie would not normally associate with, mean, older, and a guy who got in trouble a lot and smoked downtown. Richie and Billy both smoked, but never in public, and that was the difference between a good friend and a bad friend. What happened was that one day Billy was idly passing the time in study hall drawing a picture of a naked girl, copying the form of one in a bathing suit in a Coke ad on the back cover of *Life*, cupping his hand around the drawing. He did this often—he would think about girls and then a picture would begin to almost draw itself, from the meticulously shaded breasts outward.

Monk grabbed the finished picture before he could crumple it up, and while he sat there red with shame, Monk said, "Jeez, hey guys, lookit this!"

"Jesus, lookada tits," one said, growling with pleasure.

Although Billy was proud, he wondered why Monk wanted to keep the drawing. After all, he could just as well go buy one of those *Playboy*s and get the same thing. Maybe it was the contrast in the shading or something. Billy was the best artist in school and everybody knew him by that, and so his sense of satisfaction was familiar, and almost equaled the funny crawly feeling of having a picture of that kind of mind-activity in somebody's hand. While Monk showed the picture around Billy instinctively darted sweaty glances around the room for the study hall proctor, and strangely, more important than the proctor, Richie Jester. For some reason Billy didn't want him or any of his bus friends to see the picture.

Two days later, Gene Cross came up in study hall and said, "Hey, make me one—big titties, okay? Long legs?"

He liked Cross, the friendliest of Monk's buddies; so he did a better job on this one, made it more delicate and real.

Again he was surprised at the reaction. "This is great!" Gene whispered, growling with appreciation, and he put it down against his fly. "Woooo!"

"Monk's isn't as good," Billy said, more to himself than to Cross. "His had broad shoulders . . ." Cross wasn't listening.

" —Hips too narrow—you know, it didn't look real."

" 'Zat right?" Cross said.

Then another of Monk's buddies came up and said, "Hey, make me one widda nitty-gritty—make it show everything."

"No, I don't think . . ."

"C'mon, Billy," he said, looking around for the proctor. "Nobody's gonna see it." Monk stepped up, and they sat at Billy's table and made believe they were studying. "Come on."

"He says no 'cause he *don't* know," Monk said. They laughed.

"Do too," Billy said, hot with embarrassment.

"Describe it," Monk said, and then he went into imitating a teacher pointing things out on a chart. His friend's face was stretched with silent laughter. Billy watched Monk's imitation, smiling, and then Monk went to another table and got Gene Cross's picture and said, "Gonna put this on the desk . . . ."

"All right, all right, I'll do one," Billy said. It was an immense success, and a week later he did another, and another. The trouble was that each picture was better than the last, more detailed, with more background, dirtier, and then they had men in them. And each time, the maddening pleasure of doing the drawings was just barely outweighed by his studious effort to make them good. The guys wanted so many that they started offering money for them—one for somebody's buddy in another town, one for Monk of a woman and dog, another for Monk's cousin. He refused the money but filled the orders, now giddily signing the name, "Durer," because it was the only artist's name he knew outside of that guy Picasso and some Italians. The "flip book" was the biggest thing he ever did.

He worked over a month on it, in his room, making each picture almost like the next but not quite. When he put them together and flipped them slowly off his finger, the figures of the man and the woman naked in the bed moved like in a film he had seen once at his cousin's. Even though he knew that this was the worst thing he had ever done in his life, he laughed with a peculiar, sinister glee at how he could do it. The bedposts undulated a little because he didn't pay too much attention to them in the individual drawings. But the bodies moved with the natural and graceful liquid motion of living things. The woman's flesh moved with a weight—there was gravity in the pictures, and it was the resistance of flesh to gravity that made animals beautiful, he figured, and when that sense of gravity was translated into pictures, then the real thing about the animal went with it. Over his bed there was a picture by this guy Durer, of a rhinoceros, an animal that had always fascinated him. As he had seen on TV, the great thing about it was that gravity forced it to be strong enough to smoothly carry its own weight. And now the woman, with the sort of liquid jiggle, resisted gravity differently. And the man above her—when he pushed he moved her on her own flesh. He had done the pictures half instinctively, and when he finished and flipped it, he could almost not believe that he had done it.

The main problem was the face—he didn't know how to handle that, and since the only face he knew intimately was Virginia Jensen's (he knew it according to the exact proportions of the lips, the upturned nose, and the almost oriental eyes) he gave the face of the woman in the book her features, without really sensing that it was important and sometimes without really recognizing that they were her features.

The book was thirty-five pages long. Billy had to destroy about a hundred pictures that weren't good enough, and since it was too dangerous just to throw them in the garbage, he had to either deface them so badly that nobody would recognize them, which was quite a chore, or he had to carry them with him and on his way into the schoolgrounds, throw them quickly and casually into old Mr. Sorels's incinerator, which was always burning enough junk to consume his pictures before anybody could tell what they were. Sorels, who stuttered, was the custodian, and it seemed to Billy that after a week of his dropping papers into the fire, Mr. Sorels's eyes had a funny, inquisitive look in them as he fooled with his rakes and lawnmowers in the school maintenance shack. And on the last day, when the whole thing ended because of Monk Perkins's stupidity, Billy knew when he walked past the incinerator that the best and safest thing to do would be to put his book in there and get clean of the whole mess.

"I finished that book thing," he whispered to Monk in study hall. This, he realized immediately, was a mistake.

"Let's see it," Monk said, looking around toward the front desk, where Mr. Eisley, a tough proctor, sort of savagely graded tests, making thumping sounds with the point of his red pencil. Normally he taught math, and like some of the boys in school, was usually seen with a slide rule dangling like a gun from his belt. "Lemme *have* it, Cavanaugh," Monk said.

"Okay, okay," he whispered, "but I'll tell you, just look at it and put it away—don't flip it." He took it out of his notebook and gave it to Monk, who hunched his body around it. Because it was made of heavy "oak tag," which Billy had stolen bit by bit from the art room, there was a sound when Monk ran it off his thumb—*rrrrrrrp*.

Monk moaned and stamped his feet and winced at the ceiling. "Quiet," Billy hissed, breaking into a clammy sweat. *Rrrrrp*.

"Perkins," Mr. Eisley said, "stand up."

"Aww, I din' do nothin'," he said in a disrespectful servile whine. Eisley took his rimless glasses off and squinted at Monk.

"Perkins don't give me any of your garbage—go to another table and stop bothering, er, who's 'at? Cavanaugh."

"Yessir," Monk said, stepping quickly to another table. Billy looked back to his history book. *Rrrrrrp*.

"Shh," Billy said. *Rrrrrrp*.

"Perkins what've you got there? Want to show it to the class?" Billy winced. Eisley walked to Perkins's table, the slide rule swinging on his belt.

"Uh, no sir," Monk said respectfully.

"Let's see what's so interesting," Eisley said.

Monk made a good try—he gave Eisley his wallet, then his Algebra book, even some cigarettes, and finally Eisley said, "What are you sitting on?" There was a long, red silence, and it seemed that maybe Monk would just refuse to get up, but finally he scratched his head and sighed with a kind of tired annoyance. Eisley picked up the book and Billy heard the *rrrrrrp*. Eisley's face paused a moment, and then went into a mute, disbelieving daze, and finally all humanity drained out of it leaving a mask gray with speechless and inquisitive rage.

"Hain't mine," Monk ould. *rrrrrrp*. Billy got up to leave.

"Cavanaugh!"

"Sir?" He had to put his hand on the wall for support.

"Is this yours?" Then Billy had a peculiar reaction. He relaxed. "Is what mine?" he said, coolly, a studious, questioning look on his face. He was gripped numb with the clammy inevitability of the thing, but somehow instinctively he felt that he could protect himself by just asserting that he didn't have the vaguest idea what Eisley was getting so worked up about. His rage increased with Billy's aloofness. Then Billy looked at him with his eyebrows raised and said, "I don't—that is, I'm not sure I understand the *ques*tion, sir."

Eisley snorted and marched them outside into the hall. Even though he was the shorter of the two, he slapped Monk across the side of the head, and Monk drew back as if to hit Eisley, who said, "Ahh, ya . . ." and shoved him back into the room. Then Billy felt the nauseating silver flash as his head went against the wall from the power of Eisley's slap. He stumbled into the room as if he were drunk, giggling, and everything seemed bright and two dimensional, as if the whole room were a series of cartoons being flipped off someone's thumb. Everybody looked at him and whispered, and they knew that something dirty had been discovered because Billy and Monk had not been making noise. Now Eisley sat at the front of the room, still in his state of speechless wrath. *Rrrrp*. His eyes widened with shock and rested with amazed wonder on Billy.

He was sent to the principal. Walking along, Billy's aloofness barely sustained itself. Going to Mr. Baker was ten times worse than being caught by Eisley—it was absurd, in fact. There was something about him that Billy always sort of feared and respected at once. The stuffy, fatherly air, and he wore a vest, maybe that was it. It made him look like a priest, even sort of act like one. Before going into the office, Billy chuckled miserably. Here he was, facing Baker because of a bunch of dirty pictures, Baker who always talked about "citizenship" in assembly. "Did you do this Billy?" he asked. *Rrrrp*.

"Do what sir?" Mr. Baker's expression changed into a sort of confused disappointment.

"I'll ask again Billy . . . did you draw the pictures in this—this book." Billy looked at the familiar "oak tag" cover with confused but studious interest, then at the black vest which rippled over Mr. Baker's ribs. There was more red silence, and finally, dropping his shoulders, Billy looked him square in the eye and said, "Yeah, what of it?"

"Why did you do it?" Billy shrugged. "Son," he said, coming around the desk and resting his hand on Billy's shoulder, "I think you know that this kind of thing is morally wrong, and I am quite amazed at how you could have done it. I should think that . . ." and Billy's mind turned itself off to what he said, blanked itself out with the hot, trembling shame. Then Baker was saying, " . . . come in tomorrow at lunch and we'll have a talk, all right?" Then Billy found himself out in the hall.

A talk was what he expected, but when he got there the next day, his mother and father were there. "I've asked your parents in, Billy, because I think that the gravity of the situation warrants their concern." Billy's father sat there leaning forward, elbows on knees and the book in his hands and a narrow-eyed look of sad rejection on his face, as if Billy were just no good now and had to be sent back like an expensive table-saw that didn't work. Worse, he was clean-shaven, wearing the one suit he had, one with sleeves too short, so that Billy's book sat at the end of the bony arms which protruded a half foot from the sleeves. *Rrrrrp*. Just once. His mother, in her Sunday clothes, sat upright and rigid and gazed at Billy with sad concern. She didn't look at it.

"Where'd you learn this, boy?" his father said softly, a treacherous undertone in his voice. "God knows not at home."

"Jim," his mother said, "now you just let Mr. Baker . . ."

"Peeping Tom, 'at what you are?" His face was a mixture of beseeching concern and uncontrollable rage.

"Mr. Cavanaugh," Mr. Baker said, "I've asked the Guidance Counselor to talk with Billy . . ." and he went on to say that they were discussing the problem and the Counselor would be prepared to deal with it and help Billy get through this thing. Apparently, he said, Billy's associating with certain "elements" in school was partially the cause. Again, sooner than he thought he would, he found himself walking back to the study hall. This time the thing almost brought tears to his eyes, not because his mother and father knew but because the rotten sons of bitches had told them. Baker, Baker and his goddamned citizenship.

Then it seemed that they were going too far, when they got that bunch of teachers and Jensen and his father together to decide if Billy should be kicked out of school. Somehow the word had spread, and a call from a mother who found a drawing in her sons closet brought out the suspicion that there was probably other pornography. So they called their "meeting," and that brought out the recognition that it was a plump, sultry Virginia Jensen getting it from the muscular man in the book. Out of that, Billy's fifth beating. So all of it was on the table. There was almost nothing left to discover except for the other pictures, which Monk and the guys would keep secret.

There was one important trouble after that—his father became more interested in where he "got it." This meant that sooner or later he would beat it out of Billy, so the only thing to do was develop a confession like, "I saw you through the keyhole once" or something. Keep it in the family at least. Every once in a while, for no special reason, his father would blurt out, "In with the wrong boys at school are you?" and Billy would say "You know the—the elements that Mr. Baker said about . . ." and trail off, leaving any clear explanation unfinished. His father seemed embarrassed about getting to specifics.

He had got it from the house of his father's sister. Billy's aunt and uncle were away one weekend while he stayed and messed around with his cousin Stephen in Taylor, a town twenty miles away. Billy was thirteen then, two years younger than Steve. They showed a dirty movie called "The Rape," which was silent and beat-up and old. They were all drunk, Steve and his friends and Billy, and on the little screen a guy with a false nose and sunglasses chloroformed this blond woman who came home with some groceries. The stuff that happened in the film had shocked Billy—it was all so incredibly dirty, and went on for twenty minutes, in close-up, and at the end the woman who had spent ten minutes fighting the man finally ended up liking it. The light was harsh and white and the film kept breaking and the guys laughed and drank and ran the thing backwards. Billy laughed so hard that his throat was sore the next morning. But back home later that day, he sat and remembered the movie and couldn't get it out of his mind. After a while, after weeks, his memory of the movie became hazy and he forgot some of it, but certain parts, the unstaged parts of the movie crystallized at the back of his mind. And the gravity of the woman, the pull of the earth on her flesh, this he remembered best of all. When all of this popped into his mind, even three years later, the pale flesh would give him a feeling similar to the one he used to have when they sang in church and he looked at the colored windows and knew there was something to believe in behind them. When he remembered the movie there would be a momentary hollowness, a lull in the activity of his mind as if he were experiencing a vision or a recognition.

After a while Stevie became too old for Billy and he didn't visit there any more, but Uncle Fred still went fishing with Billy's father, and the families were still close. It was a movie that Fred bought for some club that they saw. After the pornography thing was on the table for a couple of days Fred stopped by and Billy heard them in the kitchen — "Why what's the boy *done*, Jimbo?" and his father explained it, with kind interjections from his mother. Fred laughed a lot, but respectfully, and every time Billy heard him laugh he would mutter, "the son of a bitch," and laugh under his breath. Finally Fred said, "Ah Jimmy, the boy's growin' up! Why you remember how we—that is . . ." and that was all he said.

The day after his fifth beating was one on which Billy began feeling almost clean. Still, the thought of what he had done, mostly the profaning of Virginia Jensen, would bring sweat to his upper lip and nausea into his throat. But it seemed near over, and now he could go back to living the normal life, watching TV over at Richie Jester's and going up to the barn to sneak cigarettes and tell dirty jokes.

The first thing that happened in the morning was that before he got to class, Monk and his friends caught him by his locker, cruelly slammed him up against it, and Monk said, "You tell 'em we got the pictures?"

Hardly able to breathe, Billy shook his head as much as Monk's grip would allow him. "Don't," Monk said, pushing his fist into Billy's neck. Then they left, and Billy stumbled on toward the Guidance Counselor's office, nodding righteously to himself, thinking that this showed him that he shouldn't have got mixed up with those guys in the first place.

Shaken up by Monk's threat, he made his next mistake. Nobody, including Billy, took Mr. Forester seriously. He was a little, sort of fast-moving guy who constantly ended up vainly trying to instruct people like Monk Perkins about sex. Perkins would come to school on Monday talking about "gang bangs" and things, and Forester would, on the same day, gather them around to talk man to man about "petting." So, Billy sat there aloof and sort of tired at having to listen to him as he explained that the pictures were "exaggerations" and therefore "distorted the truth of the thing." By accident Billy became sort of flip about it and said, "But I saw it."

"Saw it?" Mr. Forester said, tipping his head inquisitively, "How did you see it, Billy?"

"In a m—movie." At that moment he knew he was trapped. When Forester asked him where he saw the movie he said, "I can't, uh, say . . . I . . . it was just a movie at somebody's house." In the wave of frustration that passed over him, he realized that Forester would tell Baker, and sooner or later it would get to his father.

"Do you know that it's illegal to have this kind of movie?"

"Uh, I guess so," Billy said, "but, well why?" He smiled, kind of stupidly, as if the question were ridiculous.

Forester was silent for a moment, looking with calm disappointment at Billy. "Well," he said. "Because of their generally accepted corrupting influence." This aloofness was not characteristic of him. Whenever someone like Monk made a sneaky reference to doing something with a girl Forester would pass over it with joking embarrassment. Now he was serious.

"Would it have been as bad if I hadn't put her face in?"

"Whose face, Billy?"

Flushing, he said, "Uh, Ginny Jensen's."

"Yes, because ..." The bell rang, and Mr. Forester said something about coming in tomorrow and that Billy'd better get to class. Mr. Baker stopped him in the hall. "Billy, come in here," he said. Still sweating, he went in. On the desk was a pile of papers, all of them Billy's other drawings. Immediately he knew what happened. Monk and his friends had decided to wash their hands of the thing. Billy stood at attention and looked out the window and snorted, too tired to react with the proper shame. All of it seemed far away now, as if seen through the wrong end of a telescope.

"These, I assume, are all yours?"

"Yup."

"They were found in your locker."

Billy saw it in the trees blowing gently in the wind outside, saw the girl who probably found them, saw her open-mouthed look, saw her march with prim determination to the nearest teacher.

"Do you have anything to say?"

"No, ah, sir," Billy said, screwing his face up and shaking his head, and then, looking at Mr. Baker's vest, he said, "Can't we just drop all of this—can't I just quit school so we ..."

"Oh that would be a grand way out, wouldn't it?" Baker said, his voice harsher than Billy had ever heard it, "Settle all your problems that way, eh? Think that would be a good idea? Eh?"

"Uh, no," Billy said.

"This would be worth your seeing through I should think," Mr. Baker said, his voice softening. "I think you know that. I think you sense what you've done here, too," he said, pointing at the pictures. "I think you sense what you've done *wrong*."

"Uh, yeah," Billy said. "It's the putting of the inside thoughts on paper. Is that what you mean, that you shouldn't ..."

"Well, I suppose you could put it that way," Mr. Baker said, looking out the window as if thinking of something else.

"Not the thoughts themselves? Just . . ."

"Well, I suppose you could put it that way."

The final bell rang, and Mr. Baker sent him to his class, and walking, Billy had the funny, sinking feeling that he would rather just quit school. Just disappear. It was as if his life were over, and the stuffy privacy of his room, with its comics and books for ten-year-olds and useless toys, seemed inviting.

Then he heard through the din of the class change with the yelling and the slamming of lockers, someone tell someone else that it was that little kid Richie Jester who found all those dirty pictures in Billy Cavanaugh's locker. Richie Jester, who used to tell Billy about how big his sister's tits were, and how he could see her undress through a hole in the closet wall. And sure enough, when Richie himself passed by in the hall, he walked on the other side with his face straight ahead, nose up, refusing even to look at Billy. Then Monk and the other guys huddled down the hall, laughing and pointing, keeping their distance as if Billy had a communicable disease. Billy threw his books on the floor and ran at them as if to fight, and they went into their class. The bell rang, and almost magically, he found himself alone in the hollow silence of the hall.

"I'd never of told," he said. "I'd never of told." Now there wasn't anybody, on one side not to know what he had done and on the other nobody left to sort of—*say* it was all right, maybe even chuckle about it. He went to class, a bad one because Virginia Jensen was in it. All the people looked at him, but it didn't really bother him because he was used to it. In fact, the shame made him sort of jaunty much of the time. He was bad and now that this was settled, he could go on about his business. " . . . square of the hypotenuse of the . . ." Mr. Eisley said. He didn't listen. He sat down and looked around, and by accident looked right at her, and she looked at him, went crimson and looked down at her lap, with this very strange, wide grin on her face. It meant that it had finally gotten to her, through the girl's room talk probably, that it was her who Billy had get screwed in his dirty pictures. Her.

They suspended him for one week. The night of the "verdict," his father did not beat him. When they got home, they talked in the kitchen for a couple of minutes, and from what Billy could hear, his father had an appointment to see Mr. Forester sometime when Billy was out. He had found out about the other pictures, just as dirty or dirtier than his book. His father's rage was similar to his original rage, and after a few minutes he came into Billy's room, and fuming, paced back and forth. "Jeesus H. Keerist where'd you get it?" he said to his closed fist. "Where?"

And when he raised his hand, Billy cowered, saying, "At Uncle Fred's — at Uncle Fred's in a movie that he had hid in the garage that Stevie showed."

His father stood there with his hand up, a stupefied, glassy daze consuming all the anger on his face. "Movie?" he said, and his hand flopped to his side, and it was as if he had forgotten what he was saying. Then his face broke into a nauseated smile.

"Don't tell," Billy said, "please don't tell them I told."

"M—movie at Maggie's place?" his father said. "What was the name—I mean, when?"

"Long time ago . . . three years, in the garage, really . . ."

There was a long silence. His father smiled strangely again, and finally, scratched his head so that bits of grain dust which had defied the shower sprinkled to the floor. Then he sat down heavily. After a while he crossed his legs, making Billy's bed creak, and said, "Well, look, don't say anything about this to your mother, you hear?" He shrugged. "Or anybody. And—well, we'll take care of this some other time."

" 'Kay," Billy said.

They all ate supper silently, all looking down at their food. After supper his father acted funny, sort of bedraggled, like he'd aged twenty years since last week. "H'ay gad," he said, "my bones creak—work work work—seems 'at's about all a fella does any more," and then he slapped Billy's mother on the behind. "H'ay gad!" He sounded almost happy in a beat-up, wrung out way. N how mc'n ol' Rembrandt sittin' over there've gotta go out'n cut the lawn 'fore it soods."

Billy's mother turned and looked at him openmouthed. "Jim!" she said, and he said, "Awww."

Billy was to go to school for half of Friday and then stay home for the next week. He was glad about that—the prospect of his punishment didn't seem half bad. He had to work at home, but he could sneak cigarettes and his mother would let him watch television. Before he left to go home at twelve on Friday, Mr. Baker called him in to tell him to make sure and do all his assignments and that he, Mr. Baker, still thought Billy was a good boy and he had faith in him and knew he would make out all right. Then he cleared his throat and hooked his index fingers in his vest pockets and looked down at a large manila envelope. "This here is all your stuff, which I am now taking out to burn. I'll ask once. Is there any more?"

"No sir," Billy said, feeling clean and grateful.

"All right then, we'll forget about all of it then—you may go." Billy left to get his jacket, walking with a feeling of weightless exhilaration, with a sort of clean, airy feeling. By chance, on his way out of the school grounds, walking along the hedge that went to the street that ran into town, he saw Mr. Baker and the Counselor taking the bag down to old Mr. Sorels. Mr. Baker walked with his dignified gait, and behind him, almost running to keep up, Mr. Forester talked to the back of Mr. Baker's head. They gave Sorels the envelope, which he emptied into the smoldering leaves. Billy stopped and waited by the hedge where they wouldn't see him. He only wanted to get by. Mr. Baker took Billy's flip book out of his pocket, and he slowly ran the pictures off his finger while Mr. Forester watched on tiptoe over his shoulder, and then Mr. Baker threw the book on top of the pictures that were now burning. Billy had the feeling that this was something that he was not supposed to see. Mr. Baker and Mr. Forester turned and went back toward the school, walking kind of slowly. Billy looked for a place to sneak through the bushes because he was too ashamed to pass Mr. Sorels.

Then a funny thing happened. Mr. Sorels pulled the flip book out of the fire and threw it on the ground and stomped on it, looking over his shoulder at the two men walking up the steps to the side door of the school. Then Sorels shook his hand, because he had burned it. Still shaking his hand, he picked up the book and went into the bushes, his old head buried sneakily between his shoulder blades. Then he came out, walked past his fire, and went to the watertap to cool his hand.

Billy's reaction was a confused mixture of impulses—he wanted to steal his book back, felt a twinge of pride that somebody wanted to preserve it, and strongest of all, he had the impulse to run right to Mr. Baker, which he decided to do. He was breathless with righteous excitement by the time he reached the side door of the school. He didn't even consider how he would approach the subject—maybe lead them down there. "He's got it in the bushes," he'd say. "We'll just see about this, Billy." Billy turned and looked with this gleeful smile on his face.

And there Sorels was looking back, and his hand half raised as if in a plea—even though he was two hundred feet away from Sorels, Billy sensed the funny recognition between them. Sorels's posture told him that the old guy knew he had been caught. If Billy went in he'd have to go ahead and burn the book. Billy froze for ten seconds, as if resting in the relaxed jaws of an animal. Sorels sat back down again and looked nonchalantly toward the hills, as if he saw in Billy's posture exactly what the problem meant.

Imagining the look on Sorels's face when he probably flipped the book in the bushes, the surprise and the giddy pleasure, even hearing the soft *rrrrp*, Billy snorted and walked toward the gate, feeling a kind of funny blankness. For some reason he thought of the man in the book casting a delicate shadow on the woman and the shadow moving on her form like the shadow of a cloud on a hill. Best to forget about it. It wouldn't do any good to say anything anyway.

He bolstered his courage for passing Mr. Sorels. Have to do this right. It was as if they were both actors on a stage, each knowing that the other was really someone else. "Uh, h'lo, Mr. Sorels," Billy said as naturally as he could.

"H—h'lo there Bubilly," he said, his face old and unshaven and dark. "Where y' goin'?"

"Oh, I gotta go home . . . something in the family." And then he knew Sorels wouldn't throw the book away, and so it was all right. As soon as Billy was out of sight the old guy would be drawn like metal to a magnet back into the bushes. Resisting the impulse to look back over his shoulder, Billy marched down the road toward town, walking so hard that his heels hurt and feeling only the jouncing heft of his own body.

Corrigan's Progress

Only one thing bothered Corrigan's enjoyment of stalking the buck—it was the moon, with those fellows circling it, and this is what caused the accident. He had been stalking the buck an hour, through wet snow that didn't squeak, and staying downwind, he got within thirty-five yards of him probably a half an hour before dusk. Already a full moon had materialized vague and flat in the sky, with soft blue craters, and he had looked up and muttered a sullen curse at whoever did it, as if they had tinkered too much now, sending those fellows up there like that. It bothered him that at any moment as he stalked, with the bow half drawn, working from instincts developed in him before he was twelve, they were up there going round and round the moon. He had seen this on his television, which didn't have any sound.

With a sort of clumsy good luck he walked right onto the black silhouette of the buck standing between two rows of state reforestation pines. With an instinctive grace he drew the triangle razorhead arrow over his knuckle, drew it all the way back until he gently hooked his right index finger into the corner of his mouth, and judging against the oncoming darkness, he straightened his fingers and let them back in a single, fluid motion, felt the satisfying release of the bow and heard the shaft slide over the wood, the softly whistling space of time and the solid whunk—she went home.

Running up toward the buck he already knew it was his— once he demonstrated to his neighbor McLaughlin how a bow and arrow could outpower a forty-five. "Go ahead, shoot the sonofabitch," Corrigan had said, pointing at a milkpail full of heavy silt, and McLaughlin drew out his forty-five and shot it, and it sat there. Then Corrigan shot it with his bow and arrow and the arrow went through the can and mangled the metal and sent a little explosion of dirt into the air above it. McLaughlin looked down at his forty-five and said, "Keerist-amighty, was this thing loaded, or what?"

The buck lay there in the snow, trembling like a dog in a

fitful sleep. The arrow had gone through the upper neck region and probably damaged the brain. With his hunting knife out, Corrigan waited for the buck to be still. It slowed, panting with exhaustion, and feeling his stomach rise with visceral glee, he said "hah" at the moon and grabbed the buck by the horn, vaguely sensing that he should shoot him again just to be safe.

He was accustomed to accidents. In the middle of one he was somehow able to think of protecting himself, because part of his education was a series of accidents. When the buck rose explosively to its feet and ran into and past him, he instinctively held on and looked back, preparing to fall right. With the arrow in its neck, the buck tried to horn Corrigan aside.

That only bruised him, but on one of the powerful sideways thrusts the buck drove Corrigan's fist, with the knife still in it, into his stomach on the left side three inches up from the hip bone. How deep he didn't know—the angle was towards the backbone. Lying in the snow, drained of warmth and reason for a few seconds, he held the spot tightly, concerned that the leather of his jacket overlapped properly, as if this would effect the proper overlapping of his flesh. After the short span of numbness anybody feels before the brain delivers pain to a burn, he laughed with amazement, and then his voice bled out the first vicious stab of pain—"Goddamned stupid, bad oh Jesus god ... " Instinctively he looked around for his buck. "Food for the dogs," he muttered.

He stopped, feeling blood oozing toward his crotch. He could tell that the wound went in the wrong direction, into livers and spleens and stuff like that. His mind became peculiarly logical—well, here it is dusk and here I am a long ways from anybody to show this thing to. "But it ain't cold," he said. One, two miles to McLaughlin's, crosslots, easy walking, rolling hills and barbwire fences. There was another house a little closer the other way but Corrigan didn't know them and so couldn't go there.

He sat up slowly, testing for pain. It seemed to be a clean wound—that is, nothing fell out when he strained his muscle, although it hurt with a sort of rotten ache—the sting was all right, but the ache lingering in the mindless flesh under the surface throbbed ominously. He decided to look at it. He unbuttoned his jacket, and by the dim white light of the moon, saw the ripped and clotted shirt, and under that the cut. It was as bad as he hoped it wouldn't be. A gaping hole, not a neat slice. Down inside, there was the blue-gray and membranous upward bulge of an organ. Morbid interest in the mysteries of his flesh momentarily held his attention. An organ. "Oh Jesus," he said, "I really done it this time." He had to get going.

He put the bow across his back with the string bound across his chest, sort of like a sling, and with both hands pressed on the wound, he walked slowly, in short steps. After a while the blood ran down into his boot, caking on his leg with an uncomfortable stickiness. He went two hundred yards before he had to sit down again. Something gripped his throat so that he almost threw up, and he fought it by stuffing his mouth with snow. When the nausea passed, he relaxed, too tired to go on. Because he wasn't spurting blood or feeling too dizzy, he figured he was all right, that if he just trudged along, he'd make out, although he realized with a lump of fear in his throat that a couple hundred yards wasn't much for getting exhausted. He was cold now, and the snow was crusting with the night wind, and he looked up through the vapor of his breath at the white disc of the moon. "Ay you guys," he said, smiling with sad humor, "c'mon down here'n help . . ." and he thought, cause you and McLaughlin are about as far away.

"Cor'gan," he said wearily, almost comfortable in his motionlessness, "you are the accident pronest—snuk up on you again didn't it?"

He had always known somehow, down in his soul maybe, that his life was paced by an evil rhythm of fatal or near-fatal mistakes, to the extent that he had killed his girl or wife or whatever she was, racked up about every car he had and lost all of his good jobs. Something was wrong with him. He could not understand it—he was good in school and he got his diploma. Even smart, people said. In the service he got as far as a stockade in North Carolina, for stepping out of a drill formation and decking the guy who was busy calling him a bucket of crap, an incompetent hick and an idiot. He was nineteen then. With the knife wound in his belly he was twenty-nine, with a few gray hairs and wind wrinkles around his eyes.

Yeah, the punch was a mistake. Not a serious one. The thing, the invisible trickster, who had so much to its credit now, was only introducing itself then.

Back home he watched his father go bad like a dog with distemper and die, and there he inherited the fifty-seven acres and the house and the television, whose sound was already failing. And then Dora Hoag, who he met at the swimming hole, a girl he recognized from high school. She wasn't married and must have been his age, and he wondered what was wrong with her that she was still unmarried. "Just never wanted to," she said, up to her chest in the water. She wore this old one piece suit with a little skirt on the bottom. " 'Sides, what the hell's wrong with you?" she asked.

There wasn't any courting or any marriage. That same night before he ever got her back home he took her into the bush. She just went along without saying anything, and she was good. Twice more it was like that, on cold nights, smelling of old hay all around, out in the field. And then she had an argument with her parents (she had brothers and sisters and even a baby of her own which she had when she was eighteen) and came home one night with Corrigan. They had a lot of fun there, she cooking and he going out to the woods to cut logs and pulpwood. When there was work in town he would take it, but because he had a tendency to accidentally break tools and machinery, he would be the first to be laid off when the work slowed. And he would look at himself in the mirror and wonder about it, search his face for an indication that would explain it.

The worst incident was on a large hunting party with McLaughlin and four other men. By accident he almost shot one of them with a Winchester model 97 shotgun that had a funny safety catch on it. "I coulda killed you," he said to the guy, "Jeez Christ I ain't carryin' this thing." And numb with shock, he looked down at it.

"Aw it's all right, you missed me a mile," he said, laughing.

"Yeah," McLaughlin said, "you'd lose a war, Corrigan."

"I might have killed you," he said, "I'm not carrying this." They convinced him to carry it with one shell in the bottom, and he carried it, holding it away from himself like a poisonous snake. That was the last time he handled anything that had words like "automatic" on the barrel. He bought his bow then.

And now, his pain buried down there in a sinister numbness, he struggled up off the ground and said, "A knife. 'F I had a stick I'd a poked my goddamned eye out with it." It was funny. He had an ability with machines, like his car and his chainsaw, which he tinkered with and kept up. Even delicate

things: once, back in Dora's time, he had a clock that ran too
fast, forty minutes a day, and twice, on hot, buzzing July
afternoons he took it apart and put it back together again with
a jeweler's ability, it seemed. Of course it still ran fast, and Dora
would set it back every morning. It was just that machines got
the better of him sometimes, maybe because he didn't understand them. Internal combustion was a mystery, kind of awesome, although he knew how it worked. The television that
had no sound was so complex inside that he was suspicious of
it, expected it to explode sometimes. Then, the moon with
those fellers going round and round, this he would never
fathom. He knew how far away it was and what it would take to
go there and yet they did it. Hydrogen bombs was just a matter
of squashing a ton of dynamite into a thimble; and curing
diseases was just injecting these little germs into the body,
and they would fight the diseased germs and win. But this
moon thing: this was too much. He would not be able to put it
into his head. As a mystery it was too big, made all the hydrogen bombs in the world little, like firecrackers.

He didn't marry Dora Hoag, because it was too much trouble. She wasn't one for mixing with other people, a peculiar
girl he figured. Once he took her to a barn dance and she wore
a dress that was too long and wore sneakers and socks, and
she didn't look right, but she didn't care either. She just
danced and looked funny. Then a guy came up and asked her
if she meant to dance or play basketball, and so he and Corrigan went outside.

She lived with Corrigan for about a year, and they did the
same kinds of things every day. They'd go out and buy liquor
and get very drunk and then go in the car and race around on
the dirt roads, real fast, up and down the hills with the leaves
of the trees overhead streaming by, sometimes at three and
four in the morning. When it was warm they would go out in
the fields like they did before she moved in. This he would
remember: her lying like that, pale and strange in the grass
with his shadow from the moon moving on her. And they
would watch the silent television—when a guy got on there
with his microphone and sang away with the great gushy
expressions on his face they would crack up laughing. When
the newsman came on, or when cowboys argued at gunpoint,
he wanted to know what they were saying, and he would put
his ear to the set, thinking that their voices were in there

somewhere, if he could just get them and put megaphones on them. He would press his ear and hear only the kitchen clock. Once he took the set down to old Moss Hochburg, the radioman, and he said that there wasn't much anybody could do. Corrigan needed a new television set. He didn't have the money so the silent one went back home and he and Dora laughed at the singers and tried to lipread the news. This, today, is how he saw the rocket go toward the moon.

One night he and Dora got drunk and went out in the car, and he drove it into a maple tree and Dora got her skull caved in. She was dead right away, so that there was no question, her face misshapen and bleeding, and he walked to the nearest farm and called the police. Dora's father came by the house next day drunk with a shotgun, blew the kitchen window out and broke down, and all of it blew over.

Corrigan got himself a new car and sat and watched the silent television, with the sound of the clock, and chuckled at the singers, and got drunk every night. He would sit in the harsh gloom of the light from the screen, drinking away, and then he would get up and he would go out and drive the dirt roads, now in a '50 Plymouth that didn't have any spring on the brake pedal, so that every time he pushed the brake he would have to pull the pedal back with a piece of baling twine hitched to it and held in his hand.

Two months after she died, he drove into town at four in the morning, very fast, laughing as though she were there in the car, and he went into the side of a new Buick that he thought he was going past, and Corrigan was pounding the dents out of the Buick when the state trooper came. His belt squeaked and he smelled like new leather, and Corrigan thought he was his old drill instructor and swung at the trooper, who wrestled him against the Buick. The judge took away his license for good and fined him for driving drunk, for driving without insurance, for driving an improperly registered car, for assaulting an officer of the law, and for not appearing in court on the right day.

It was like a recovery from a sickness, his living at the house for the next year or so. He worked in the feed mill where all he did was carry feed, and McLaughlin became his only speaking acquaintance. He dropped Corrigan off at the mill in the morning, picked him up at night, and they went hunting now and then. And every year McLaughlin would buy a new car,

and once in a while he let Corrigan drive it down to the hard
road. You just touched your foot on the pedal and the damn
thing pressed you against the seat with its silent power. When
he drove McLaughlin's car he would do it with great care,
slowly, both hands gripping the wheel, which you could turn
with one finger. Once he suggested that they take the cover off
and adjust the valves, and McLaughlin laughed and said,
"Can't touch 'em."

"Why?"

"War'ny says that if you tinker with the motor, like adjusting
anything, then they won't guarantee it any more."

"Can't even touch your own motor?" Corrigan asked,
amazed.

"Nope—can't say as I care to either."

At home when he had time to think, Corrigan would have
the funny lump at the back of his throat, wondering why
nothing seemed to come out right. He spent a lot of time
speculating on what it would be like if he'd somehow not hit
the tree. These were elaborate reconstructions of all the time
since she died, and lasted sometimes for hours. It seemed
strange that all of it hinged on a momentary clumsiness.
Sometimes, late at night, thinking like this would drive him
out to walk along the roads, and once, going crosslots, he
made it all the way to town and went to the graveyard. When
he found the stone he said, "Hey," and chuckled and looked
around at the dark gray stones and the black grass. Then he
shrugged and left.

And now, at twenty-nine, a little more gnarled and tough
than he was at twenty, he plopped down in the snow for his
third rest, looked up at the moon and wondered how he could
have done all that he had done and now have the knife happen. He knew he shouldn't have tried to slit the buck's throat
like that. Anyway, he thought, at least it was just me that got
the worst of it this time, and maybe I'll die finally, and there
won't be any more question about it. Like the judge, who said,
"We just can't let you drive, that's all." Maybe that was the case
with his life. And it seemed almost attractive, the prospect of
dying, just dumping the whole thing. He had been going the
wrong way anyway—backwards. He remembered the picture
on the television, of the gleaming precision of the dashboard
of the spacerocket, with the men there throwing their

switches with the efficiency of machines. Christ, how incredible that seemed!

Dully he got up and trudged on, not feeling particularly weak, but the pain bothered him. It was as if he had eaten something foul. He didn't know how much blood he had lost, but he could feel it squishing in his boot. He walked and walked, maybe a thousand yards this time, looking down at the crusted snow, his wrists aching from gripping the wound. The snow forced him to high step, and for long stretches it would support him and then give out on one step, and he would fight his way back up on the crust in a blind rage, screaming out his curses in the direction of the moon.

On his next rest he realized that he had gone in the wrong direction and had to backtrack two hundred yards to a creekbed that he figured ran to McLaughlin's property. More crusted snow, this time deeper, and when his foot went through he would sink in to his thigh. "Sonsofbitches!" he once bellowed, shaking his fist at the moon, "Who do you think you are?" In silence he would glance up at it with grudging comtempt, as if the men up there were somehow responsible for the state he was in.

Finally he threw up, bile scalding his throat and mouth. He lay in the snow in a semiconscious doze, drained of his anger. He imagined what it would be like, just floating around the moon, with the earth off there in the distance, and for a moment he had the absurd vision of Europe, with Britain in red, France in green, Italy in yellow. He giggled drunkenly, realizing that there wouldn't be any dotted lines or colors. Just a ball, slowly turning, white and green and blue. He had a sort of dream, of McLaughlin passing by in his car as Corrigan lay there wounded in a ditch, and McLaughlin saluted from the window like the guy in the TV ad who just bought a new car, and Corrigan stayed in the ditch, lying on his side, humbly accepting the fact that McLaughlin didn't pick him up.

He woke up a little later very cold, feeling raw and sore, and the inside of his mouth burned and his teeth grated against each other, and when he tried to get up, he seemed to have no strength. Then he broke into a sweat and the pain ballooned throughout his body, and his stomach heaved convulsively as though more were coming into his mouth. He bellowed for McLaughlin, feeling the wound surge under his hand.

It didn't let up, and he looked at the sad face of the moon or the lady with the sticks on her back and figured that the ground was going to claim him now, swallow him up, and for a moment he thought he should say he was sorry to somebody, because now he was scared. He should now apologize. Who? Nobody. He thought, maybe God, but instead looked up at the sky, figuring where the rotten old son of a bitch might be, and gave him the finger. Then he waited, almost tried to submit, to will it to happen. The pain just got worse, and he got colder. He relaxed his grip on the wound, and caught a whiff of it — a funny, sort of tangy decay, like the hot-guts smell of the slaughterhouse. That smell made his flesh react. It became slick with fear, and in a ponderous, drunken frenzy he got up again, fighting against the cold and slimy discomfort that movement caused. He scuttled his bow, violently dashing it against a tree.

His progress was slow, a yawing, interrupted stagger, awkward and mindless and the woods and fields he had known since he was ten became an exasperating maze of dead ends and counterfeit shortcuts. Each time he thought of quitting again, he would remember the smell of his own guts and his flesh would crawl with nausea. He made mistake after stupid mistake, once managing to cross his own tracks. Familiar-looking paths enticed him and betrayed him, fences he knew he had built led him to quarries and creekbeds he knew he had never seen. While he groped, back and forth, over one fence and another, the weather got worse and the moon went behind a cloud. Then he was moaning almost unconsciously with his exhaustion, blindly lumbering across a field lashed with sleet, and ended up draped gasping over another fence, the iron-tasting saliva gumming in his mouth. This time it was an electric fence with the power off.

Half aware of its significance, he muttered that it had to be McLaughlin's since he was the only one who had an electric fence, although Corrigan could have been in the next god-damned county for all he knew. No, it was McLaughlin's. All he had to do was decide in which direction the house lay, and numbly he turned to the left, walked two hundred yards and found himself standing on a knoll looking down at McLaughlin's house, with the new car parked next to it. Corrigan cackled idiotically—he probably made it. Staggering on toward the house with a clumsy, joyless determination, he thought, so I get another chance. McLaughlin would take him to a doctor, who would sew him up and put that stuff that smelled like antifreeze on the cut. Nearer the house Corrigan sensed an ominous silence — where're his dogs? "Hunting," he said. "My god, he's out coon hunting!" Yup, there were tracks, man and dog.

Again wild with fear he got inside McLaughlin's car and looked for the key, thinking he'd drive to town. Not in the glove compartment, the ashtray. His fear woke the pain up and he trembled uncontrollably, running his hands over the seat and floor, not holding the wound. The key was under the floormat. He plunged it at the dashboard, searching for the ignition, his hands numb and barely able to hold the key. Finally he slumped back giggling, and settled. No use.

As it turned out McLaughlin found him around dawn, sitting nearly frozen in the car, the key still clutched in his hand, and tough as he was, Corrigan was still alive, muttering away in weary exasperation, gesturing with the key. He seemed to be saying something about how it wasn't his fault at all, that it wasn't ever really anybody's fault, that he, Corrigan, had figured out that it wasn't hardly anybody who was good enough or fast enough or smart enough for all this. And he seemed to be saying it to the cold and confusing elegance of McLaughlin's dashboard.

Sacrifice

Later he would think it was the third year. Or it was because it was the third year. And then that strange three-day span between the morning of the rescue and the afternoon McGarty rushed him to the hospital, his hand wrapped in a blue towel with little fish pictured on it—that three-day span was all nausea, and his mind was tumid with sensation.

And there would also remain in his mind the picture of four objects in a line, one of which was the lifeguard's chair he was required to sit on that morning. He sat and gazed dully at the brownish water, watching the girl swim back and forth, thinking, why the hell does she want to swim on a day like this? Isn't there something better for her to do? He twirled the whistle on his right index finger as he had done so often during the summer, so that now the skin was polished and almost without prints, a perfect ring above the first joint. But for this woman he would be in the shack playing chess with McGarty.

The beach was deserted on either side. To his right was the bloated Pekingese lying in the shit line, looking like some beached aquatic mine from the Second World War—and there looming in the gray fog to his left was the south tower of the mammoth bridge named after Verrazano. Three objects then in the picture: Verrazano Bridge; his orange chair, property of the City of New York Department of Parks; and the Pekingese partly buried in the sand. He recognized possible meanings in this lineup—dog half buried, the chair—yet the final significance of the three-object picture eluded him

He saw it coming, saw the process of the creation of the fourth object. Was already standing shaking his head, feeling that strange urgency rooted in an even stranger inertia: a massive black piling from a Monsanto dock or from the splintered stalls of the ferries moved with ponderous assurance through the water like a half-submerged submarine, the little ineffectual waves lapping against its butt. She swam toward it without opening her eyes and his mind worked on the image of the closing gap: veer left, lady, for Chrissake look up!

He put the whistle to his lips and rapped out the short two-blast warning. Nothing. "Hey!"

Still nothing. He glanced around at the shack, but since, after choosing this unlikely day to swim, she had chosen the edge of his beach, the shack was two hundred yards off. She swam on and, yes, went head-on into the piling, which continued at its normal pace as she slipped under it. He laughed, expecting her to come up spluttering, scratching her head. When she did not come up he did what the book told him to do and what he had practiced a thousand times in the three years he had had this job. He blew the long burst on the whistle, jumped off the chair, ran along the beach until he was directly in from the place he last saw her, and entered the water.

He would barely remember the instinctive search, the first contact (an ankle), and the process of dragging her in. He did this with mindless energy, with complete assurance, and without fear.

It would take him fifteen minutes to find that he had sprawled the semilimp form between his chair and the dog. The mindless process continued: arms down at sides, the little push at the base of the ribcage to clear the throat, her mouth filling with vomit and blood. He turned her face sideways, toward the chair, ran his fingers into her slick mouth and pulled out its warm contents, straightened her head, went full lips to lips, and with his own tongue pushed hers out of the way and began the resuscitation. Her chest rose slightly, and he rose, spat out the blood and half-digested breakfast into the sand, and went down for the next breath.

On the fourth she still did not respond, so he blasted on the whistle between breaths to bring McGarty from the shack. But he knew the problem: this air was thick with moisture and seemed to have the properties of a soft solid, a kind of jelly. The blast of the whistle could easily be lost in it. Still no response.

God's artistry is subtle, he would think later. Twenty-four hours after the incident he grills McGarty about it, first describing to him the picture—the bridge, his chair, the girl, the dog—and saying, "Weird, eh? Where were you? What took you so long?"

"In the shitter. Watch your queen."

"What were you doing there?"

"What do you think? Reading a magazine while ... "

And Dave's mind works at this new information.

"Was it a skin magazine?"

"Yeah—come on, you lost your queen. Take the move back."

There Dave cackles with nervous laughter, remembering.

Because the self-consciousness that comes with long participation in any activity came to him at about the twelfth breath. He rose from the cold mouth, and spat something into the sand. Rice, soft grains of rice. He got ready for the next breath and saw her. Age, maybe his, twenty-one or so. Face not beautiful but nice. He noticed too with a peculiar horror that he had placed his hand on her breast without thinking. The two-piece bathing suit had slipped its strap off one shoulder, yielding to him the soft and somewhat small mound of pale flesh with the nipple in the middle. When he went down again, this time moving his hand under the breast, he saw against the water the perfect silhouette, a little black square of nipple rising off the breast, and he began to sweat through the drying salt water. Up again, after the blast of the whistle, he looked down once more. Body B-plus. Short legs, the soft belly with the perfect little line of brownish blonde hair disappearing into the bottom of the suit, and away from that the plump and delicate crotch. Down again.

Still laughing: "What else were you doing?"

"What?"

"Of course," he almost shouts. "You were. You were beating your meat."

"Aw come off it."

"You could just as well have been ... don't you see?"

"No. I don't see a goddamned thing."

Oh yes, he thinks, there is a simple perfection in all this. She didn't have big breasts! Of course—that would have been overdoing it. More would have been in bad taste. "Yeah yeah—just beyond, beyond whatever, there is a meaning whose clarity is staggering."

Laughing, shaking his head, McGarty says, "You're outta your ass, man."

The seventeenth breath, eighteenth. He continued, blasting away at the whistle, wondering why no one saw them. The sweat was pouring now, and he was nauseated by the taste in his mouth, by the rancid odor around him, by the foulness of the air, by the degrading filth that this beach collected. Even the goddamned sand was half cigarette ash, it seemed. He began checking her pulse then, and found only what seemed like an erratic beat, weak. Noticed too, that some sinister force had made him place the girl between the dog and his chair, and the nausea rose in his stomach—the absurd chance order of the four-object picture hit him then, and the taste in his mouth would have been the same if he had tried to revive the dog.

He thought, girl, I breathe life into you, air, oxygen, breath by breath. What can I do to make you respond? Why the fuck don't you respond? Awkwardly he pulled the strap back over her shoulder and went up to blast the whistle.

When did the figures appear? Much later—as he hovered on the edge of vomiting, all the while bathed in rancid sweat, going down for breath after breath, the blood and bits of rice and strings of mucus rising in her mouth, each time finding no difference in her body's response, except for one hopeful moment when he pushed her tongue off to one side and she bit his finger in a peculiar, almost gentle reflex. But the limp features, the slack jaw, the eyes showing slivers of white, reduced the face to a corpselike relaxation. And the limpness suffused her whole body. If jostled she would jiggle with useless lack of tension. It took the figures so long to appear that he grew angry at her refusal to respond. He hated her. Mixed with the anger were insulting images. Once on TV he had seen a bull elephant try to revive a dying cow by mounting her. Would that make you breathe? Thy belly like a heap of meat? You with your snooty coquetry refusing to live regardless of what I do? He rose to yell, "Goddamn sonovabitch!"

And saw McGarty, struggling his way with the resuscitator in slow motion because of the heavy sand, his form offset by the weight of the case, and then came the distant wail of a siren. Dave screamed "Hurry" and went down again, now seeing forms running his way from Midland Beach, the next one down the line, the larger one where the crowds went. McGarty came swearing, "Oh Christ almighty, goddamn, Oh Jesus . . . " and undid the case, opened the valve on the bottle and jammed the little finger-shaped cage of wire into the mouth to keep the tongue out of the way, and then slapped on the mouthpiece. Dave crawled away toward the water, hearing the hiss click hiss click of the machine, and let his stomach have its way.

He made no assumptions after they took her away. He remained in a warm cloud, hardly hearing the voices of the younger lifeguards from Midland asking him what happened, what happened? They pestered him until he finally threw his hands up and yelled, "Get that fucking dog off the beach. Get it off now!"

They used sticks and a plastic bag, all working in his peripheral vision, muttering, "Hey, there's a bullet hole in its head." He heard the swish and plump of the dog being dropped into the bag and immediately smelled the result of its being disturbed from its rest.

A bullet hole.

"What do you want us to do with it?"

"Jesus Christ! What to *do* with it? What to—*Jesus!*" He looked at them gazing back at him with suppressed humor, insolently feigning respect and attention. "Take it up to the shack and see if you can *revive* it. Put it in my *locker*." Laughing, they walked off.

He could talk to them like that—he could yell at them. "Animals," he muttered. At twenty-one he was considered ancient, after three years he was considered boss almost. Him and McGarty, who had asked the lieutenant for Ocean Breeze instead of Midland to let them off easy this time, to permit them to waive responsibility for the avalanche of flesh that came to them from the bridge, to let them off from the business of breaking up fights, ejecting drunks, keeping people inside the lines, mediating disputes over squatters' rights to trivial patches of sand. He would think of himself as over the hill—poor Dave, who recognized somewhere along the way that the people in the water were his responsibility, that rules were not to be broken, that all people had to be watched, protected from their own stupidity, that disaster hovered everywhere, even when one guard watched one swimmer. Poor Dave who would permit anything only two years ago, who once even sat on his chair and rooted for a kid who seemed to be drowning in the midst of a multitude splashing around him. Dave sat leaning forward, silently urging the kid on, nodding, saying come on, come on kid, attaboy, and the kid finally did make it, and Dave leaned back and twirled his whistle. And who on Parks Department time would take the chicks under the boardwalk (c'mon, nobody can see, nobody walking up there is gonna look through a goddamned crack, and off comes the top, and standing behind her he puts a hand on each breast and watches himself move them on the pale chest until something silver glitters through the air and plops into the sand just as his right hand has made it inside the suit bottom, and sure enough the kids want to know where their quarter went—hey there's Dave, whoooeee! and the girl is gone, swearing back at him).

Now they come, he thought. *Now* they decide to come. With the sound of the siren hardly gone, the people began to arrive, the kids, the little loud-mouthed and familiar regulars who like to hang around his chair because he gives them swimming lessons on off times. The Midland refugees loitered, waiting for a report on the girl.

"Look," he said, "since you're gonna hang around, let's draw in the lines. I gotta clean barnacles. It's been a month since we ... "

"Okay," they say. "Sure, why not?"

A little black regular watches. "Get some shovels ... we'll dig up the deadmen."

"Where the dead mans?" the kid says.

"They're not really men, Brillo, " Dave says. "They're logs that hold the ropes. We just call ... "

"They ain't no dead dudes down there," he says, his eyes wide with angry suspicion.

"No there aren't. They're just logs that we hitch ... "

"Hey I seen the chick went away in the amblance—she dead?"

"No Brillo, she's not. She'll be okay, she'll be okay ... no sweat."

"Well she *look* doad."

The huge ropes lay coiled behind the shack. Dave felt tho coolness of the shade and decided it would be all right to do the ropes for the rest of the day. He would place a machete in the crack of the old log, blade up, and then hammer the barnacles to pulp on the ropes. Then he would take the rope, section by section, and scrape the rest off on the upturned blade of the machete. Except for the fishy smell of the barnacles, it wasn't a bad way to pass the day. But first he had to play McGarty for the privilege.

McGarty won again but, feeling guilty for the time he spent in the shitter, volunteered. "I'll sit—go ahead with the ropes."

"Thanks brother. Tell the Midland boys to go on back."

Two hours later he rises from the log, his hands slimy with pulp from the massacred barnacles, and faces McGarty, who has just said, "She never regained consciousness. Fact, she was already dead here."

"What was her name? No, never mind, never mind."

Night, wide-eyed in the velvet absence of stimuli, he thought, under my hands. In fact, died while locked lips to lips, the awry bathing suit strap unnoticed, the delicate mound of breast—if McGarty had looked from the shack what would he have seen? What could he assume? Only that Dave sure had a lot of nerve doing that in broad daylight.—Why me? What the hell did I ever do to deserve this?—In the air, faintly, he could sense the dog, or maybe it was the residue of the barnacle flesh on his hands. Even his mother noticed it and forced him to put lemon juice on to nullify the smell. Yes, that smell, a sign, like the white dust of his father's work clothes from the sheetrock company he worked for. The smell went with him through the night.—She died under me. Love you to death—While McGarty was in the shitter slamming the ham over—In dying she takes half my life with her. Good not to know the name. Jesus Christ—fix it for all time if he knew her name. She expired on his breath, blown into her from his own lungs, already partially used, like the smell of air blown into a paper bag or a balloon. He felt the pulse, he did feel the pulse, therefore she died under his hands, died while being asked to, at least temporarily, use his breath to sustain her until—H'm not bad looking, not too stacked but what the hell, anything you can't get into your mouth is excess anyway.

And in the morning, the interrogation. "Where were you? Why didn't you hear the whistle?"

And what lay in the shit line when he walked it this morning? Dead dogs? People? Beached submarines? No. A ham, complete with strings, looking for all the world ready to cook. Into the bag it went and, turning, he saw the people begin to come in. Brillo was fourth.

"Did the chick die?"

"She did, she did." Nodding.

"I *knew* it," he said. "I sure did know it. She look *wasted*."

The progress of this is subtle. Dave is barely aware— hovering behind him somewhere, or all around him, by day and more by night, there is something awesomely nauseating, but barely distinguishable. It resides in the shit line, a vapor that rises from it. Whatever it is, it puts him on guard. Even Brillo sees it: "Who you waitin' on, man?" and McGarty, who is astonished at how clumsily he plays chess during off times.

He endures another night, as if his life if over—under my hands, locked lips to lips—almost sleepless, the vision of the girl, whose lungs still hold residues of his air, slackening toward her own decomposition, the features stretching and loosening toward the earth. He sees it all in the black mirror of his bedroom window; all light is a trivial flash in an immeasurable oblivion and he has sent his breath into it.

Another day, gray with moisture. He does the ropes, feeling raw and disembodied from lack of sleep. His vision is two-dimensional, fuzzy, annoyingly bright. He smashes the barnacles with the mallet, swinging with angry force, scrapes the rope on the upturned blade of the machete until his hands drip with the viscous slime of the litte animals. He goes to wash his hands every twenty minutes. McGarty invites him to chess, but he refuses. He prefers wallowing in the stink of his job. The air, the heavy, sweat-stimulating moisture of it, exaggerates the aura of aftertaste everywhere. It is now, with that wretched feeling of disembodiment, of nonalcoholic hangover, that he acts with brutal quickness. He hardly feels it.

McGarty drives him to the hospital, glancing down at the towel with obsessive frequency, his face twisting in vicarious pain.

It was almost a week later that he admitted to McGarty that it was no accident. "What?" his face a mask of disbelief.

"I did it on purpose," he said, smiling.

"Why?"

He chuckled, yawned. "Well, the truth is I don't know."

He didn't. He knew only that he slept that night and had slept since, slept easily and with a peculiar peace. An act committed without awareness almost. When it was over he ran toward the shack holding his hand, and then McGarty led him out of the shack while the Midland boys ran down the beach to take over. He realized only in the car, with the towel wrapped around his hand, that he had placed his index finger on the upturned blade of the machete and struck it once with fierce assurance, leaving a joint and a half in the barnacle pulp on the log, the mallet cleaving tightly to the machete.

The Drive

He stood in the path that his grandfather had broken in the thigh-deep snow, the blazing slits of his vision crossed by the old man's form. The wind seared the right side of his face, and his muscles were already sore from being tensed against the cold all morning. He had no idea where they were.

"Pete!" the old man yelled. "It's the highway!"

"Christ it's about time," he mumbled, squinting into the distance. He could just barely see it through the swift clouds of snow streaming south. "My God!" he said. "Hey!"

"What'd I tell you?"

"I believe it. I believe it."

"Never. Not even in fifty-seven was there one like this."

Lined all along the northbound lanes were cars, trucks, semis, some jutting in various angles into the lane the drivers had tried to leave free for what traffic could make it.

"Calloway's is three miles up that way," the old man said.

"We'll never make it. Never," Pete said in a high-pitched, quaking voice. "Jeeheesus it's cold!"

"Nonsense," the old man said, drawing out his flask. "Snort?"

"No. Listen, we can't drive them through this. 'Sides, we don't even know if they're alive."

"Ahh!" the old man said, smacking his lips. "Oughtta have a slug boy. Put hair on your chest rather'n those sweetie locks on your head." He laughed, then went into a brief, explosive coughing fit, spraying brown tobacco spittle into the snow.

"I tol' you a thousand times," Pete said to the bent over and wheezing old man, "everybody wears long hair. None of your business anyways. Listen . . . ."

"Them cows ain't dead," he finally said, resetting the wad of tobacco in his cheek. "Calloway left 'em outta the wind."

"But there's no way we're gonna drive them through this. The highway maybe . . . those trucks make a snow fence kinda. But . . . ."

"Cows may be stupid but they got thick hides. That old bull is still alive too."

Pete smiled, remembering the bull. A year ago he and his little sister Chrissy named him Malt Liquor, and the name stuck. It almost gave this stupid trip the shadow of a meaning. "I'm for goin' back right now," he said. "This is ridiculous."

The old man turned and faced the highway. The ancient Iver Johnson single-shot twenty hung on his back suspended by frayed baling twine. It was for the lame cows, to put them out of the misery of bearing their deaths in this weather. "Well I'm goin' that way," he said, looking at the glittering surface of the unbroken snow before him. "Your brother, he woulda been walkin' in front of me." Pete groaned, thinking, that old line again.

"All right, all right. Here, let me bust it for a while." Movement was agony—it woke up his body, made him realize how cold his feet were, and his hands, icy and tense balls of fists closed inside the palms of his gloves, so that the leather fingers dangled empty. He trudged ahead, sending little explosions of snow off his knees. The crust deep underneath was not quite strong enough to support him, so he could not establish a rhythm in his exaggerated goose step.

"Listen," the old man said, "if we can find a spot where there's any kind of ridge going down to the highway, we can drive them on it. You know, any kind of rise. Snow'll be blown off it. Better if it's right around here since there ain't any fence along the woods we came through."

"OK, OK. Let's get to the highway first."

The snow had caved in Calloway's barn, killing half of his cows, and then a spin-off fire gutted his house. Grampa's idea to bargain for them was based on his conviction that Calloway had wanted out all along. Old friends, he and Calloway had one opportunity to deal over the phone before that went dead, and Grampa emerged the owner of the remaining sixteen cows and one bull, in trade for fifty acres of land he never used anyway. Calloway would grow potatoes from now on, set himself up on the insurance from the loss of the house, barn, and stock. Calloway told Grampa that it wasn't much of a deal unless he came and got the cows in twenty-four hours. Otherwise they'd be half-dead. Grampa told him he'd be there with bells on. Pete's mother wasn't pleased about the idea. She railed at her father as he sat and serenely chewed away on his tobacco.

"Just tryin' to keep us off the welfare lines," he said.

"Well you're not going," she said, hands on her hips.

"I am too. I'm your father and what I say goes."

"Grampa," Pete said, "she's right, she's just trying . . ."

"Why don't you get a haircut?"

"Stop evading!" she said. "You're too old! It's eight miles! The snow's . . ."

"Or a permanent," he said, and laughed himself into a coughing fit. Pete's younger brother Danny came in followed by Chrissy and their old dog. "Can I go too?" Danny said.

"Listen, I'll keep an eye on 'im," Pete said to his mother. "Maybe it isn't as bad as the radio says."

"I give up," she wailed, and turned to the sink.

The old man would not change his mind. Pete spent the rest of the evening living in secret dread of the trip to get the cows, not out of fear but out of the simple recognition that they would not make it in this weather and the old man was dreaming. The only other problem was that they would go on Sunday and he would miss the NBA basketball game of the week.

To the family the old man was a perpetual embarrassment. He seemed coarse, at least compared to other people they knew. He had a tendency to look dirty even though he was clean, because he wore old clothes and rubber farmer's boots . . . shirts faded where his back was slightly humped, crossed by the nearly white straps of ancient denim. His hands were gnarled and battered, and his hair was pepper gray and thick, and then there was his most insufferable habit, tobacco chewing. The corners of his mouth were stained with it, and drips would stain his shirt and the stubble of his chin.

In an old glass case in the living room were set up a number of little ornate black boxes with gold framed tintypes of his ancestors—hard and angular men and women with eyes as flat as tin and seemingly angry expressions on their faces. Pete had spent long periods of time before the case, staring into the faded pictures, especially at the bleached eyes, and sure enough, Grampa had them too, kind of washed-out blue discs with the black points of pupils in the middle. The family had been in the same stone house for over a hundred years.

Their farm sustained itself on land they rented to other farmers and ten cows. Grampa's idea to add seventeen to the ten was to him a new start, and to Pete and his mother nonsensical regression. They thought that producing milk was becoming obsolete for anyone who had less than fifty cows. There just wasn't enough income. Grampa maintained that Calloway's were the best cows around, and the problem was that theirs were nearly scrubs and too old. Another problem was that bad times had left them shorthanded. Years ago Pete's father got fed up with life in the boonies and left them flat. Then Pete's older brother Sonny was killed in Vietnam, shot through the heart in a firefight according to the soldier who visited them after the news came. Pete was eleven, and after that, whenever he saw a cop or a cowboy go down on TV his mind would flash that image of his brother, whose features were as familiar as his own, going down clutching his chest, with bright, Vietnamese jungle in the background. But about being shorthanded, Grampa was not concerned. Boys grow up. Pete and his mother bombarded him with reason all the way to that moment when he stuffed a wad of crudely prepared sandwiches into his pocket and threw the shotgun over his shoulder and walked out into the driving snow.

In the silent hollow created by the looming form of a semi, Pete stamped the snow off his legs and boots, feeling light with the sensation of no longer being held back. A mammoth drift had obliterated one side of the truck, and ten feet off the other side the snow was less than a foot deep. Above, the snow floating in the sky swept southward and swirled off the mushroom on top of the truck in a slow, almost horizontal tornado that dispersed into the sky.

"Somethin's wrong," the old man called from the front of the truck. Pete jogged over to him, loosening up. The door window of the tractor was broken and the interior had been sprayed with green metallic paint.

"Who the hell would bother?" Pete said. "Kids I bet."

"Looks like they took the guy's CB out too," the old man said. The back doors of the next truck had been jimmied open. Lying partially drifted over in the road behind the truck were new color television sets with their screens shot out.

"Quasar," Pete said. "And all we got is a black and white."

"Don't get ideas. I'm wonderin' what happens if they come back. Kinda glad we got this old shotgun."

"They aren't gonna bother us." Unconvinced, the old man shifted the wad of tobacco across his mouth and grunted.

Pete shrugged and walked through the fog of his breath to the next truck. There they found cartons of books overturned in the snow. The old man picked one up, opened it, and squinted in disbelief. "There ain't nothin' in it!"

It was called the *Write Your Own Book*, bound in expensive-looking imitation leather with gold lettering. Pete laughed and flipped through the pages, trying to manipulate them with numb fingers encased in cold leather. "It's a new thing."

"Suppose anybody buys somethin' like that?"

"Yup." The old man's eyes narrowed with angry suspicion.

"Well what the hell for?"

"Shh, listen." From way off, down the line opposite from the direction they walked, they could hear a motor, high-pitched, quickly varied from full throttle to idle. "Plows?"

"No," the old man said, "not a tractor either."

Then they heard the bang and echo of a firearm. "Looters."

"Means they've been down there all this time? Don't seem right. Somebody'll catch them for sure." The old man chewed, listening. "But then the plows'll take all day to get here. Gotta come from town, eight miles. Let's get goin'. Prob'ly be gone by the time we bring 'em back this way."

The vandals seemed to have no basis for selection of vehicles to hit. There would be an untouched Cadillac, then a Ford with broken windows and decorated in green paint on the inside, then untouched trucks, then a van relieved of half of its contents, various kinds of stationery ... a card at Pete's feet read, "Sad to hear you're down ..." along with a picture in rich and warm colors of a basset hound whose ears dragged on a marble floor.

Soon they passed the last truck in the line, and fought their way up the slope on Calloway's side of the highway. The old, rusted barbwire fences were mostly down there, and would cause them no trouble. By the time they reached the top of the slope the weather had calmed, leaving them trudging, blinking in an awesome hush, the only sound from deep in the sky, a soft rumble of powerful weather high up. Now able to scan the blazing horizon without having his face slapped by the wind, Pete felt the full sense of the monstrous purity of snow ... fuzzed at the surfaces by wind or razor sharp in its definition, it rounded the shapes of all things into gentle curves and voluptuous billows, even when covering twigs. It even had a smell, kind of clean and desolate and metallic.

He became fascinated to the point of being barely conscious of anything else in his observation of the snow, until off in the distance he saw through the bright slits of vision the cluster of black and dirty white forms, the cows. No barn. He turned to the old man, who looked drawn and tired. "Somethin' wrong?"

"Slowin' down, boy. Brightness gives me a headache."

"Well, you've proven that you're human then. I'm pooped."

" 'At there is Calloway's," he said, forming his hands around his eyes. "Wouldn't know it would you?" Calloway's house was half-gutted, and inside all the floors were iced over. Pete skated across the living room, watching an old floral rug pass under him through an inch of ice speckled with a suspension of soot and ashes. The barn was in its own foundation, and the cows were grouped behind it out of the wind. Calloway had left hay for them. Malt Liquor came around the pack, head high, vapor blowing from his snout. Pete could feel his walking in the ground. Calloway's old dog Bucky rose out of the drift he made while sleeping in a ball, growled, then whined to them and shook the snow from his coat. "Jesus, he left his dog too."

"Don't seem right does it," the old man said. He went and patted the dog. "Hey old fella," he said.

One of the cows, a little Guernsey, had freshened either the night or the day before. She lay on her side in a snowbank nearly dead. The calf was sitting in amongst the other cows, looking like it wouldn't last either. Grampa tried to get the cow to stand by lifting at the base of her tail, but she was too cold and too weak, so he gave the shotgun to Pete, who shrugged, aimed, and the Guernsey's head snapped into the snow with the impact. Spooked, the other cows rose and looked, the vapor from their snouts curling into the wind. Grampa checked over the calf and determined that she was OK, and decided to take her along. "But we gotta carry her 'cause if we sling her over a cow she'll die for sure ... can't take all that jostling on that bony spine."

"Grampa come on," Pete said. "Cows is one thing, but ..."

"I ain't askin' you to carry it," he said.

"OK, OK." Pete found some feedbags in the rubble and folded the calf's legs under its belly and put it inside a double bag. Then he made a hood for it, and to warm it up, gave its back a vigorous rubdown through the burlap.

They found one other cow in the rubble, pinned by a huge beam and still alive. It would lie for a minute, blinking at nothing with those huge liquid eyes, and then raise its head to fight the beam. A four-inch thick splinter of wood had been driven through her side, and icicles of blood hung from it. The old man shot her, and the beam settled.

"Been holdin' that wood up all night. Poor lady."

"Are there any others under there?" Pete asked.

"Might be, but we can't take the time to get to them."

"Grampa, I'll take the snort now."

"In the afternoon the heavy snow'll come back," Grampa said, handing him the flask. "See those clouds up there? It's comin' now. We'd better move on."

Pete choked a little on the whiskey. "Y'know," he wheezed, "we could build a shelter right here. Whooee, that burns."

"Wouldn't be a bad idea 'cept we don't know what the weather's gonna do. I'd just as soon get 'em home."

"Well, it's your game. I'm just along for the ride."

They slapped rumps, and after a brief balk, the cows started down the driveway, Bucky snapping at their heels. Grampa tried to pick up the calf but couldn't.

"I'll get her," Pete said.

"Well," Grampa said, smiling.

"You knew I would all along." Pete put the calf up on his back and wrapped its stomach around his neck, holding the front and back legs in twos on his chest.

Even though Malt Liquor could break the drifts easily, he was so long-legged that the cows still found themselves held back by the snow. But for each one that made it, the trail was clearer for the next. It took them about an hour to angle down the slope to the line of vehicles. Luckily there were no guard rails to negotiate. Pete struggled along behind the last cow, winded because of the fifty or sixty pounds on his back. They were just back on the highway, stamping snow off their boots, when they heard that motor again, high-pitched, gunning and letting off, down toward the other end of the line of vehicles. "Hold up," the old man said. "What do you think? More like a chain saw than anything else."

"Listen, I'll take Bucky up ahead and look. You rest."

"Thanks boy. I could use it."

Pete trotted in the direction of the motor, Bucky running far ahead of him. As he ran, Pete envisioned snowplows, men clearing, exhaust smoke. The eerie atmosphere of the scene was oddly frightening, because of the absurdity of the fact of how much had been left. There was an almost dreamlike improbability about the idea of new color television sets turned garbage in a snowbank. He slowed to a walk, winded. The dog went on, stopping to sniff at tires and then racing ahead. Then he too stopped, looking in the direction of the drifts ahead. Pete could tell by the set of his body that he was growling. There was a high-pitched roar, and then a drift about sixty yards away exploded, and through it came a man riding a bullet-shaped thing on short skis. Snowmobile. He wore a ski mask, so that his crimson face had two round eyes, no nose, and a round mouth out of which trailed breath vapor. He stopped the vehicle when he saw the dog standing there with the hair up on its back. Pete waved and walked toward the snowmobile, but the man didn't see him. He inched toward the dog, pointing.

Bucky was blown against a truck tire. In the dying sound of the shot Pete's mouth filled with the taste of copper and he turned and ran, and the man on the snowmobile revved and followed, quickly decreasing the distance between them. Then he suddenly gunned and turned back. Grampa stood in the road aiming the shotgun. Pete tripped and fell at his feet, gasping, the iron-tasting saliva thick in his mouth. "The sonofabitch shot Bucky!"

"C'mon, let's get back this way."

Back with the cows Pete sat in the snow trembling, his heart thumping in his chest. He couldn't talk yet.

"I figured it out just when you ran off," the old man said, keeping his eyes on the road ahead. "Radio said there was looting, and I figured that whoever took all those TV sets and cards and empty books or whatever was here still, 'cause they can't get out. Know what they're doin'?" Pete gasped, shook his head no. "'F you wanted to make a little money all's you'd hafta do is get a good truck with a blade on front and zip in here after everybody left. OK, they did that, but remember last night? That was one of the worst this week. Nobody coulda seen that comin'. If they coulda left they would've. Now they're scared, 'cause when the Cats come to bust us out, these guys is caught for sure."

Panting, Pete looked back into the northern sky. "Jesus, Grampa, nobody's gonna bust us out today . . . look up there."

You could see it coming, like a white tidal wave above the horizon, and squinting, you could see that it billowed high in the sky, slowly consuming the limits of your vision.

"It's called a whiteout," Grampa said with a strange excitement in his voice. "That's what the news said . . . up in Buffalo, why Jesus, nobody could see three feet. That's what's comin', a whiteout."

"Hey, there's a half-empty semi up there. We could put the cows in there."

"No way to get them in. Half'll break their legs. Let's get them in the hollow behind the first big truck there. If it's a high wind they'll die sure—frostbit bags and noses. Gotta get them outta the wind." Pete looked. He was right. The cows' bags dangled under them, pink and engorged with milk. They drove the cows into a space between two trucks, bordered on the side away from the wind by an immense drift and on the other side by nothing.

It took long enough for the heavy weather to begin that they had time to worry about the snowmobile. The old man leaned against the fender of a nice Diamond T semi and squinted into the distance. Then the wind increased and the thick snow began to swirl and blow until it lashed their faces. By then it was useless to worry about the looters. They were socked in between the trucks, looking out at a plane of white that streamed by at a speed making the vision surrealistic. The cows stood immobile with heads lowered, the snow swirling down on their backs.

Grampa decided that they should milk the cows into snow . . . wasn't a good idea to let them pack it in like that. Have all kinds of trouble—mastitis, vets, medicine. They hunkered in amongst them and squirted the steaming milk into the snow. For a few minutes Pete's fingers felt like exposed nerves, until the exercise warmed them. He squirted milk into the calf's pink throat and made her stand to get the blood running and keep the milk down. Then they kicked out a hollow in a drift and sat down against the front tire of the Diamond T, Pete with the calf next to him.

"Could be in for the night," Grampa said, nudging Pete with his elbow. "Holsteins are tough though . . . don't you worry."

"No way. I told Ma we'd be back before sundown."

"Well, we couldn't see this happening. Gotta go slow."

"You're just enjoying the hell out of all this, aren't you?"

"Keeps the blood runnin'."

"Senior citizens' activity day."

"Don't get snotty."

"I saw that look in your eye, when the snow was comin'."

"No, actually I was a little scared."

"Aww."

"No kiddin'."

When he finally had the opportunity to stop and think about it, Pete threw his head back and laughed. "My God," he said, "look what you got us into! Guys with ski masks shooting dogs, us next prob'ly, blizzards, all for what? Cows?"

Grampa said nothing. He grunted and drew out his flask.

"And look there. You're getting drunk too."

"Don't sass, boy. Don't slow me none. Keeps a fella warm." He took a little swig and said, "Them cows is worth four, five hundred dollars each. Bucket and a half, more some. I tell everybody a hundred times, these are twice as good as ours. Don't you get the, what's the word, economics of that?"

"I get one big pain in the ass."

The old man looked at the cows, thinking. Pete became restless and stood up, looked around, shivered and sat down again. The old man nudged him. "You chase the skirts in town much, do you?"

"Now what the hell kind of question is that?"

"I was just makin' talk. Do you? Chase the skirts?"

"Yeah, so what?"

"I did too, your age. Guess it was different then, kinda more formal, you know?" He thought, chewed. "What do the girls think of the long hair?"

"Christ I don't know. What kinda question is that?"

"I'm just askin'." He nodded slowly, looking distant. "Sonny sure got in a lotta trouble chasin' the old skirts."

Pete chuckled, then looked away. He couldn't figure out why the old man was so interested in talking about this now. It seemed out of place. "You got a girl friend?"

"Yeah, off and on."

The old man nudged Pete again. "Actually I don't care about the long hair. I'm just funnin' you. 'Sides, makes you look kinda like a blue-eyed Indian when you wear that leather thing. Better'n nothin'."

"Grampa? Hey, what're you getting at with all this?"

"Ah nothin'. I was just wonderin' what you're up to is all."

There was a ruckus at the edge of the little herd. Pete jumped up and pushed through the cows. One at the outer edge had locked her upper foreleg in between the bumper and body of the Diamond T, up by the shoulder, and the wind was throwing her against where she was caught. The old man worked his way through, holding the Iver Johnson over the

cows as if he were walking through chest-deep water. The
wind outside the hollow lashed Pete's face with a piercing
sting and he could hardly keep his balance, and he thought,
now wait a minute, this isn't real. This is too much. "Bumper's
tearin' her up!" he called. He put his shoulder against her and
tried to shove her out. She was almost hanging from the
bumper and the sharp corners of the inside tore deep into the
muscles.

The old man shook his head. "Half ripped off," he said. She
tried to run into the wind and yawed around and knocked
Pete down, then tore loose. When the wind caught her broad-
side she blew over and slid in the snow, belly up, about ten
feet. She tried to rise, but the dislocation of her shoulder made
it impossible, and she went over again and slid out of their
sight. The old man went out into the wind, leaned back into it
so that he was walking at an angle, and he too disappeared
into the plane of mottled white. Pete experienced a flash of
sick fear, looking at the spot where the old man's form had
vanished. He might never come back. They both could die out
here . . . it came to him that the crazy old man had lured him
into an exile so foreign to anything familiar that town and his
house and friends might as well have been ten thousand miles
away in some different world. It was the snow . . . it lulled
them, altered their reason. They were toying with obliteration
and it made no sense. He had to get himself and the old man
out now.

The shot reassured him. It came from very close, a flat,
almost echoless crack, the sound absorbed quickly like everything else by the snow. Grampa came back, fighting the wind,
walking like someone negotiating a steep hill, the shotgun
held out in front of him as if it were a rail. "Jesus God I ain't
seen anything like this all my life!" he said when they were out
of the wind. "Ooooee!"

"How long's this gonna go on?"

"It's twelve-thirty now," he said, gasping for breath. "Sun
goes down in four hours. Oughtta slow off at dark. Least that's
the . . . way it used to be. Night not as bad as day. Man!"

"Ma's gonna be madder'n hell."

"Boy," he said, slapping his knee in exasperation, "you got
to understand that we ain't playin' around here. Letting good
cows die is stupid. 'Sides, she's *your* mother, not mine."

"Calloway didn't think much of them leaving them like he
did."

"That's his fault. He only wants the insurance."

"Well, it ain't worth getting killed over."

"We couldn'a seen this. I didn't say it'd be easy."

"Well, then we shouldn'a done it. This is crazy."

"When it gets too easy then it ain't worth much."

"What ain't worth much?"

"*Nothin'* ain't worth much. Christ, I may be seventy, but things look awful funny to me. Look at all that stuff— TV's, trucks, people sprayin' paint on stuff for no goddamn reason *I* can figure, books with no words in them. What a waste." His face was twisted with a look of deep disgust.

Pete laughed. "Aw Grampa," he said, "you're some old boy, you are." He shook his head. He'd just have to wait the old coot out, wait till he got tired. "Hey, I'll have another snort, that is if you haven't drank it all."

"I got another just in case."

"I'd a figured. You got those sandwiches in your pocket there?"

Pete gave up on talking him out of it now, and they ate the sandwiches, occasionally venturing out into the wind to see if it was dying. After a while the old man struggled up to his feet, looked around, placed a gloved finger next to his nose, and snorted into the snow. Pete chuckled, remembering a school open house where he did that, right at the front steps, kind of delicately, pinky extended. Pete's mother was so furious that she could hardly speak, and when she did, in a harsh whisper in the hall, Grampa stopped, held his hands out and said, "I forgot, I forgot!"

"Ain't any sense in sitting around," he said. "If we go now, maybe those fellows won't see us."

"What about the cows?"

"Sniffle." Pete did. "Nostrils don't stick any more. There ain't that chill in the air now." He looked around. "Let's wait a little. This is gonna thin out."

The old man stood at the edge of the wind, watching for the snow to thin out. He broke the shotgun and pulled the slug out, hefted it to feel its load, and put it back. As if that act had invented it, the sound of the motor came through the wind. "It's him again."

Still here, Pete thought. A creep with a pistol. "Grampa this is ridiculous. We gotta get outta here, get home."

"I ain't gonna let them mess with my cows."

"You seen too many movies."

"Boy, you go home and you live with it if you want. Besides, you don't know what he wanted with you. He didn't see you. Mighta wanted to apologize for shooting the dog."

"I wasn't gonna hang around to find out, I'll tell you that."

He thought about it again, that coppery taste in his mouth, that awful, dreamlike feeling of being chased by something faster than yourself. Behind that was the vision of his brother, too, falling, holding his chest.

"Let's go," the old man said. "I say drive them along until we find a spot where the snow looks blowed off, and run 'em up. I'm tired of sittin' around."

Pete looked into the blowing snow. There was a certain, rubber-legged inevitability about the whole thing, and he needed a minute to set his mind to it. All right, you goddamn old fool, he thought, gesturing at the cows with a hopeless flap of his hands. He went back and got the calf and threw it up on his back and held the legs in twos on his chest. Then he nudged the cows out of the hollow between the trucks.

Grampa was right. The visibility was up to a hundred feet now, and as they drove the cows slowly, Grampa in front holding the shotgun as if he were hunting birds, it seemed as if the line of trucks and cars extended gradually in their vision. They passed the dead cow, then the drifted-over form of Bucky, then the book truck. The wind pushed them, so that the cows' tails streamed in the direction they walked. Then they were beyond the TV truck, and Grampa slowed between each set of new trucks—there he would pause, look, and shake his head. Interested, Pete walked on the truck side of the cows and found a van that had carried liquor splattered with cheap wine and floored with broken glass, then a truckload of naked manikins, pink and thin women with lewd decorations in green spray paint, their expressions showing no awareness of the violation or of the cold, and stranger yet, pale and muscular men with no genitulu.

"I see it!" Grampa yelled back, looking over the hood of a burned-out car. Pete walked to where he stood, at a point where the line of cars and trucks began to curve gently to the right. You could see where the hump probably was, and then where beyond it the snow curled and drifted. The grading had a soft ridge in it, running from the highway up the hill, probably a place where a storm drain was buried. The wind kept the snow level and shallow on the hump. Beyond the top of the hill was woods, then pastureland, then a pine forest and familiar territory.

And then Grampa was looking off to his right, and as Pete turned, three figures materialized out of the blowing snow like a photograph in a chemical solution. All wore ski masks. They looked and gestured. Grampa raised the shotgun so that it crossed his chest. "Well, there's our friends, Pete," he said. Behind them was a small truck, its open back doors showing cartons stacked almost to the ceiling. It was dwarfed by the last semi in the line of vehicles. Beyond that was their problem: the highway dipped, and you could see that the wind passed over the dip and left it drifted over, probably up to ten feet in places. Pete was further surprised to find that Grampa's prediction was correct—sure enough, one of the wings of a V-shaped plow blade jutted up from the hood of the truck.

They stood and regarded each other from a distance of sixty yards. Pete numbly considered the predicament they were in . . . him with the calf slowing him down, Grampa with the old shotgun.

"Look at the snow behind them," Grampa said. "You see any more of them skimobiles?"

"Looks like only one."

"Can they go over deep snow?"

"Wherever they want." Grampa looked up the hill at his intended route, considering. Pete knew what he was thinking . . . they could chase, harass, spook cows.

He could see them moving around the small truck. One man trotted to the front in a peculiar, slow-motion gait, lifting his legs too high as if he were running uphill, unsure of his balance. "Something wrong with that fella?" Grampa asked.

Pete looked, wondering. Then he laughed hoarsely, his chest hurting because of the weight on his back. "He's looped."

"No wonder," Grampa said. "All that booze they took."

"No, stoned, Grampa, stoned. He's as high as a kite."

"A dope fiend?" Pete nodded. Grampa's face twisted into a look of curiosity mixed with fear, and he stopped chewing. "Well I'll be dipped," he said. "We're in trouble now."

"Nah, he ain't gonna bother us."

"You don't seem worried about that. You ever taken dope?"

Pete laughed and said nothing. He hadn't, but he didn't want to admit to that, even to the old man. At Central High it was something only the seniors did.

"All right," Grampa said, with the sound of warning and disappointment in his voice, "let's get the cows past the dope addicts." He shook his head, looking at the shotgun. "I seen everything now . . . dope addicts on skimobiles goin' nuts over books with nothin' in them, greeting cards. Jesus."

Then two of the men by the truck began laughing, so hard that in a short time they were bent over holding their stomachs, and one finally fell into the snow, out of control. The third walked away from them, shaking his head and gesturing at the deep snow blocking them from their escape.

"What's so funny?" Grampa asked.

"Beats me." One man got on the snowmobile and started it, and lurched toward them a few feet. Grampa raised the shotgun and aimed in the sky above his head, and he stopped.

"Now hold on there whippersnapper!" the guy yelled, imitating a western accent. "You got a burr in your saddle 'ere shodbushter?"

"You gonna head 'em up and move 'em out?" the other man screamed, and banged the wall of the semi next to his truck.

"Let's go," Grampa said. "Don't say anything to them."

Pete was numb with fear again, but the weight of the calf on his back kept his mind off it. He nudged the last cows and Grampa poked Malt Liquor with the butt of the shotgun. The man who did not laugh now stomped around, talking to the other two in an intense but unintelligible whisper. They paid no attention to him.

Past another semi now, doors open, revealing large cartons in which were washing machines, dryers. Another van, this one filled with scrap wood and tools, and on the floor in the back frozen vomit, caught by the cold in the act of running off into the snow . . . brownish-yellow icicles. Pete turned away and looked at the men, larger in his vision now, forty yards away.

The next happened too fast for him to react. The snowmobile did a quick turn, throwing a fan of snow into the air, and came along the highway at a fast clip with the man hunched down and bouncing as the vehicle plowed through the irregular sweeps and small drifts which crossed the open lane. He had the gun in his hand. Grampa shot into the sky and yelled, "Git that thing away from . . ." because the cows spooked, started to slip and jostle in the little herd while Grampa fumbled in his coat for another shell, and as the vehicle passed the man gave out a whoop and shot straight into the herd. The sound was like a baseball bat against a hanging rug, a deep thwock! and one of the cows raised her head and slipped in the snow, regained her footing, and walked on. Grampa aimed and the man skidded around and went back to the truck, and then pulled across the lane behind the last semi in the line. He didn't want the old man shooting at their only way out.

"Turn 'em into the snow!" Grampa yelled, "Right here, these trucks!" Pete trotted out and around the herd, nearly exhausted. Malt Liquor plunged into the snow, heaving his body up and off his hind legs and breaking forward. Grampa watched the last semi in the line as Pete poked the cows into the broken drifts. Then he flipped the shotgun on his back and kicked his way in behind the huge form of the bull. Pete poked the cows into the space as it cleared. Then there was another crack of the pistol and a bong of the bullet hitting metal back down the line. Pete kicked the last cow in and then high-stepped into the snow and fell, struggled up again, still with the calf on his back. When the herd was off the highway and hidden from the sight of the looters, Grampa worked his way back to Pete. "Hold it. Listen, they got us here if they want us."

"So? Let's go."

"I was lookin' back. Looks like the men are in their truck now, and that skimobile is parked behind that last semi. You take this shotgun down there and blow the works outta that little thing and we're home free."

"Not me. C'mon, if we just hustle. . . ."

"Look what they done," Grampa said, pointing.

The wounded cow stood with its head lowered, and pink foam dribbling from its nose. The little hole in her side did not bleed. "She's finished," Pete said, again vaguely thinking of Sonny with the hole in his chest.

Grampa spat tobacco juice into the snow, his face colored with his anger. "All right then I'm goin'."

"Wait, wait. How do you know they're in the truck?"

"Well I saw two of em go, from up the hill there."

"Where's the third?"

"I don't know, but from up above there I could see the skimobile. When we get part way up that hill in all that snow out in the open, we're sitting ducks."

"Why would they bother?"

"Don't ask me to tell you how a dope addict thinks." Pete sighed and shrugged. It almost didn't make any difference now. He was too tired to care. "You just go along the trucks, peek around, and put a hole in that thing. Then we'd be OK."

Pete looked at the sky. Half the reason they were in their truck was the snow. It was on the increase again. He took a deep breath, getting ready. "OK, OK." He unloaded the calf and Grampa gave him the shotgun, nodding with satisfaction. Hefting it, Pete looked at him. "You look tired," he said.

"You worry about yourself, boy."

Pete nodded. "OK, if I don't make it, send Kojak."

He worked back to the trucks and walked along in the deeper snow on the other side of the line from the open lane. The effort of fighting the snow kept him from feeling the fear he knew he should feel. If his assumption that there was only one snowmobile was correct, then they'd be OK if he disabled that. But he couldn't help feeling that he was destroying their property and they had every right to get mad at him.

When he emerged from behind the second to the last semi he saw the snowmobile about forty feet away down the wall of the last truck, close enough for one shot. Feeling a mischievous tickle in his stomach, he aimed for under the rear of the bullet-shaped body at what looked like operative guts, and let fly. Even before the pieces of metal and tubing that exploded off the thing disappeared into the snow the third man appeared not ten feet from him, across the open back of the semi behind which he had been hiding.

"Dad!" the guy yelled, frozen in place. Pete broke the shotgun and felt his pocket, but Grampa had the shells. The guy pulled off his ski mask, probably to see beter. He was about Pete's age, his eyes bugged out with fear. In that strange moment of peculiar inertia where they studied each other, Pete glanced the thirty yards at the end of the loaded truck, and heard a door open. He had to go through the kid ... it'd take too long to work back along the deep snow behind the trucks. He even had time to notice the lucidity with which he plotted his next move, and behind that, the flash of recognition that he was even enjoying it. He jumped out of the drift and closed the shotgun in one act, then turned it and held it like a baseball bat. The kid had apparently been plotting with some of his own clarity too, because he suddenly swung the open door of the semi at him. Pete ducked just as it did its screeching arc and banged shut.

Both seeing that the first step was complete and they were still crouched and eyeing each other with that combination of lucid focus and tense-backed excitement, they paused one more millisecond and lunged. Their contact was brief, almost gentle. He shoved his forearm into the kid's throat and got a painless glancing blow off the forehead. After that he ran in a fast crouch out to the shallow snow. The kid did not chase. He yelled "Dad" again as Pete ran along the trucks and around the end of the one where they turned the cows into the snow. Running up the path made by the cows, he laughed, feeling light, exhilarated. Grampa had apparently watched it all and was now carrying the calf and urging Malt Liquor on, and the bull rose and fell, rose and fell, straining powerfully against the snow.

Running, Pete expected to hear shots, but none came, so by the time he got to the last cow, the wounded one, he stopped and looked around. The kid was trying to stop the other men from chasing . . . he held them back, talked to them. Finally the men went and looked at the snowmobile, and the kid turned and looked up in Pete's direction. There was another strange moment. From fifty yards, vision dulled by the flying snow, he could see the vapor of the kid's breath, the set of his arms, hanging out and probably tense with the cold. He wasn't sure why he or the kid looked, except that circumstances had led them into this combat and they had both emerged without a scratch, neither the loser.

"Grampa!" The old man turned, the vapor of his breath coming in quick gasps. "Put her down. I'll get her. This one's finished." The wounded cow would no longer walk. The pink foam at her muzzle bubbled into golfball-sized spheres in which Pete could see the tiny black reflections of himself, and now blood was leaking from the corners of her mouth and out from under her tail. Grampa came back and handed him a slug.

"They're not following. Hey, I saw you down there boy." Pete aimed at the lowered head and pulled the trigger. The cow's body flopped on its folded legs and relaxed into the snow. The three men scrambled for cover. "Shame," Grampa said, looking at the cow.

"You walk behind," Pete said. "Take it easy."

The drive up the two hundred yards of highway bank took a long time. The snow was deeper than Grampa predicted, so they moved at the rate of a few feet a minute, and every step was exhausting for Pete because of the calf . . . the weight made him tense his body in an unnatural leverage as he leaned into the snow, and his hands went numb from being up. The higher they went the worse the wind blew . . . the cows instinctively turned away from it, and they had to bat and punch them back on track. Grampa would kick, bellowing, "You goddamned stubborn jackasses—that way! That way!"

Near the top and the woods the snow shallowed and the wind decreased, and Pete groaned with the pleasure of being able to stand up straight. He turned to wait for the old man and saw him sitting in the snow by the last cow, doubled over. He rested the calf on the snow and went to him. "Grampa?"

"Got me a pain," he said through his teeth. "Chest."

Heart. Pete froze, looked around. They might as well have been on Mars. He bent down and reached into the old man's coat for the flask. His face was ashen, and he looked stunned, distant, and inwardly contemplative. Pete opened the flask and held it to his lips. "Take some, then rest. We'll leave the cows there in the trees. If you can make it a little more we can go on home."

"I'm all right," he said. He took the flask and drank some more. "I just need a breather. We'll get 'em home. We can't leave 'em here. Die for sure."

"No, I'm takin' you home. Me'n Danny'll come an' get 'em."

"If I gotta walk, then I might just as well let the cows bust the snow for me."

"Listen." Way off in the distance to the south they could hear the sound of powerful diesels. "There's the plows."

At the line of trucks the little one with the blade was moving now, backing up and driving into the drift over and over. "They're gettin' ready," Pete said. "No way they'll make it." He felt his forehead. The kid had apparently hit him harder than he had thought.

"Funny," the old man said, "now I'm wonderin' what we're gonna feed these ladies . . . hardly enough grain'r hay for our own."

"Weather clears and we'll buy some, with the money we make milking these."

Grampa laughed at the tone in his voice, then coughed, spraying tobacco juice. "Should I slap your back or something?"

He shook his head. "S'pose the . . . the weather don't clear?"

"It will. It always does. Don't worry Grampa."

"Just figgered, you know, twenty-seven cows, no, twenty-four now, and these fourteen as good as you'll ever see. . . ."

"Don't worry. You were right all along. Ma, she don't. . . . Well, she worries about other things. A good cow is a good cow, like you say. We'll be in fat city."

"And I never would of thought those dope fiends down there'd shoot at us. I didn't mean to put you into . . ."

"It's OK. I kinda enjoyed shooting that little thing. Serves 'em right. Hey, you cold?"

"No. But you coulda been shot. I saw you fight that guy."

"It's OK, really. It was kinda fun."

"God, when I think of Sonny thousands of miles away with his head blowed off. . . ."

"No, heart. He was shot in the heart."

Grampa paused, squinting into the distance. "Well, you're old enough I guess. That friend of his told you and your Ma he was hit there because. . . . Well, I'm not sure why. Truth of it was that he had no head from the lower jaw up, and that he accidentally got in the way of a grenade meant for an officer, in his own army yet."

"There's a word for it," Pete said, before the full sense of it hit him. No head. A grenade meant for. . . . He knew the lie was important, but wasn't sure why.

"You were just a kid," Grampa said. "Guy said he looked around at you and your Ma and figured he couldn't say it and that was all." He shook his head, a sort of dazed look in his eyes. "I never could tell her neither. She's had enough trouble without having to figure that out. Boy'd never hurt a flea." Grampa drew out the flask. He still looked worried, almost sad, but the color was returning to his face.

"Hey, I'll have one too," Pete said.

"Hell, I don't wanna cause trouble, and it seems I always did. Your Ma, she thinks I drove your Pa off . . . truth is that he's a no good son of a bitch and we're well rid of him. She even thought I drove Sonny into the army, and that. . . ."

"Don't Grampa, don't. You know Sonny, nobody could drive him to do anything he didn't want, 'cept a girl."

Grampa laughed and drank from the flask. Pete stared into the snow, wincing at the thought of it . . . pieces of face flying outward from the explosion, the body dropping.

"Just don't seem right to let good cows die," the old man said. "Let them other folks do it, wander off and wait for the goddamn insurance check, leave cows to die, trucks all over the place. Seems like nothin's worth savin' any more."

"Yeah." The old man slowly chewed his tobacco again, and arced a ball of brown spit into the snow. "Whole world's always been in a mess," he said, "but now it's in a mess that don't make no goddamn sense." Now he chewed like his old self. "I don't care what the hell they leave down there, whether it's TV's or books with no goddamn words or mountains of gold or whatever. These cows is ours . . . ours is all we got and goddammit we're gonna keep it and look after it." He shifted the wad of tobacco across his mouth. "I just don't figure it." He moved to get up. "C'mon, I'm OK."

"Throw your arm up over my shoulder."

"No I'm all right. You get the calf 'fore it freezes."

"OK, now you take it real easy," he said. "Real easy."

In the woods the wind hummed in the treetops, and it was dark enough that Pete could open his eyes instead of seeing everything through those blazing slits of vision. "Now where are we?" he called back to the hunched over and trudging form of the old man.

"We angled way off goin' up the hump, so we go that way, maybe a mile." He pointed into the wind.

Pete nudged the bull. In the shallow snow they made better time, but when Pete turned to check on the old man again, he didn't see him. He dropped the calf next to a tree and ran back. He was doubled over again, seemingly retching. "Oh Lordy," he said, "I got that pain again." His face was pale and waxy and he looked stunned.

"I'll get help. You sit still."

"No wait. I just need . . . we'll be . . ." He raised his head to continue and could not, and then stared at Pete with a kind of curiosity and astonishment at the failing of his speech. Then he went over on his side, eyes glazed.

"Grampa!" Pete rolled him over on his back and shook him, but he was limp, his eyes showing slivers of white. He pushed on the old man's chest and the tobacco fell out of his mouth and lay steaming in the snow. "Listen, we'll get you home," he said, and took off his own coat, removed his outer shirt and tore it into strips, and tied them together into a rope, his hands fumbling nervously. Then he got Malt Liquor, picked the old man up, surprised at how light he was, and draped him on the bull in a riding position. He tied the old man's limbs together under the bull's neck and chest, hoping that it was docile enough to carry him without balking. He put his coat back on with quick, outward punches, and nudged the bull.

Struggling under the weight of the calf, he worked along the ridge in a kind of mindless refusal to accept the worst, expecting the old man to wake up any moment. Frequently straightening the old man up on the bull's back and speaking to him in short sentences—"Easy, now, just hang on"—he drove the cows for about half an hour looking for land he recognized. It seemed like the longest mile he'd ever heard of, but he figured he had to hit the pines sooner or later. Near dusk he went to Grampa to straighten him up and brush snow from his face, and found when he touched it that it was as cold as the shotgun wobbling on his back. He had to accept the simple fact that he was dead.

He put the calf down and sat in the snow and experienced a feeling of timeless inertia ... the world was over there somewhere, and he and the dead man and the cows were on the desolate edge of it. Sure, back there were some looped crooks, eight miles away people watching television, five miles up, probably, a 747 going south, but this little group of lost and freezing flesh was too remote to mean anything any more.

The only thing that kept him from staying there was discomfort, and then he supposed he had to keep going simply because of how far they had come. He went to pick up the calf and peeked inside the burlap to make sure it was all right, and saw its eyes staring back at him—bottomless wells of ancient patience and complete lack of comprehension. He threw the calf on his shoulders and held its hooves in twos on his chest.

In his haste to drive them into that patch of land he would recognize as the gateway to home he forgot Grampa, and found him slung by his arms next to Malt Liquor's neck, his head wobbling limply and his body in the grotesque parody of an embrace. Muttering with embarrassment, he righted the old man and tried tightening the pieces of shirt to secure him better, but the numbness in his hands made them almost useless. He noticed too that one of his boots had ripped, exposing part of his right foot so that he felt snow packing in the crooks of his toes, and the discomfort of that made him limp and grunt under the weight of the calf.

Just as it got dark enough that he could completely relax his eyes, he saw the conical shapes of pines heavily laden with snow ... the woodland bordering the pasture they had crossed that morning, only two hundred yards away. Beyond that it was still a long way home, but at least now he had something to go on. He drove the cows across an open section of the ridge toward the pines, and the snow and wind lashed his face, took his breath away. Blinded by it, the cows straggled, their tails streaming in the wind. Pete trudged back and forth, trying to keep them together. In his moaning exhaustion he worked blind at times, stumbling close to unconsciousness, sometimes falling face down in the snow and thrashing back out, cursing ferociously.

Inside the pines the density of growth nullified the wind. Above him it roared in the treetops, but where he stood gasping, the metal-tasting saliva thick in his mouth, there was that awesome silence, broken only by the whoosh of air from the cows' nostrils and ears flapping as they shook the snow off. He knelt under a cow and squirted milk into his mouth. It was now dark enough that he would have to depend on memory rather than sight. He humped the calf up on his shoulders and his knees buckled and trembled. He was not sure if he could go another ten feet, but went anyway, through the dense pines, whipped by the hard, thin branches, and then out to pastureland and the mottled sheet of streaming white which seared the side of his face. He drove them by memory and instinct, sensing that ahead of him, beyond the white that was now almost black because of the darkness, the magnetic pull of the warmth of his house directed him. He trudged along on feet numb beyond pain, forgot the weakness of his legs, which now pumped in slow and tortured mechanical cadence, to the front to push the bull, to the back to kick the stragglers.

He drove them to a draw he recognized as the one he had played along all his life, and turned the cows into the wind. One of them fell in and broke her front leg, so that when she rose to follow, the last ten inches flopped ahead of her and she dropped down to limp on the splintered stump. Trying to make his hands obey him, he clumsily aimed the shotgun and dropped her in the draw. Again Grampa embraced Malt Liquor from the side, and Pete went to straighten him up.

He was awakened from his mindless stupor when he reset the body. His hand fell on the old man's face, and through the gloves and the numbness he could tell that the surface of the flesh was frozen. The sensation of crackling ran into his hand like a subtle current. Gazing at the old face, the snow en-crusted eyes and mouth, he felt his own face break and he cried like a boy. It lasted only a few seconds, and he stopped, his mind clear with a strange, pinpoint lucidity. He looked at the blowing snow, the iron-gray sky, the dim forms of the cows, and then stumbled over to the calf.

He got the calf to his shoulders and rose unsteadily from his knees and staggered on into the inky-gray field of vision. After that, trudging from the front of the line to the rear, half-conscious in his exhaustion, he had no sense of how much time passed. It seemed to him that he was covering vast plains of snow, but he didn't question it. He was aware only of the dim shapes of his own knees appearing in his vision against the snow as they pumped in their agonized and patient rhythm. Now the old man hung on the side of the bull, but Pete did not have the energy to do anything about it any more.

Had the house been farther away, then he would have gone to it, but since it was there, very dimly lit in the windows, he approached it and the weight of the calf made him fall on his face. He struggled out from under her and rose to his knees but they would no longer support him. Then the figure of a woman emerged from the house carrying a kerosene lamp above her head. It was his mother, running out to him balancing the lamp in a shifting circle of yellow light, and for all he knew the vision could have been a dream . . . it was as if he had come home in the nineteenth century.

He remembered later that before he was helped to the house his mother saw Grampa and screamed "Papa!" in the shriek of a twelve-year-old girl, and ran to him. Hours later he was aware of voices above him, of someone crying, and the familiar pitch of Chrissy's voice. All through his sleep, late at night, there was the odor of the kerosene lamps, and a sound, something like a slow and reassuring heartbeat that he could not identify, because he was not sure where he was, and in his exhaustion he didn't care. The gentle beat went on, behind every vision his mind conceived . . . Sonny with no head, the blast of a grenade meant for someone else, flying bone and hair, his grandfather frozen in the grotesque embrace of the bull, violated manikins unaware of the cold. When he woke up later he realized that the heartbeat was the sound of the rocking chair his mother sat in above him as he lay sleeping on the couch.

He sat bolt upright. "The calf. Where's Danny?"

"They're all OK. He's in the barn. You rest. You've got a couple of frostbitten toes. They should be. . . ."

"Where's Grampa? Was he frozen?"

"No, only a little. We put him in his bed."

"Danny's gotta keep the calf warm. They can't feed it yet."

"He knows. You rest."

"Be sure of that. She'll get sick if you give her too much right off. There's some of that dry stuff in the . . ."

"We know. We have that all figured out. You rest."

In the early morning the blizzard continued with as much force as the day before and the week before. According to the transistor there was no let up in sight. New records were being set every day. Pete talked over the sound of the radio, telling them what happened, sitting with his foot up burning and tingling. When he ate he could hardly hold the fork—his hands shook from the accumulation of fatigue from the day before. His mother told him that Danny and Chrissy had left at three yesterday afternoon to bust their way out toward the pasture to look for them. They heard one shot, way off, after sunset, and returned home. At home they waited three more hours, until almost ten o'clock. Pete's mother waited for the phone to work to call the police, because she heard on the radio that looters were on the highway and people were advised not to go near abandoned vehicles. A number of people were found frozen in their cars up north a few miles.

Later they heard one story about their section of highway being cleared, at least long enough for the police to get to the looted and damaged vehicles. One truck with three men in it burst from a drift and raced off to the south, and the police gave chase as well as they could, but the looters and the truckload of stolen goods disappeared altogether. When he heard this Pete turned away from the rest and found himself gazing into the bleached eyes in the tintypes, and his mind cocooned in on itself. So they made it. That kid shaped them up and they busted out. It was strange, but he felt a peculiar satisfaction that the kid had escaped.

After that there seemed to be no more to talk about, and it became clear that their electricity was staying off for a while. Pete rose from the chair and went for his boots. "Where're you going?" his mother asked.

"Just the barn. Gonna check out our new cows I guess."

He put the right boot on carefully, trying not to irritate his toes. Danny and Chrissy jumped up and went for their coats. "You feel all right?"

"Yup. C'mon you guys, let's go."

"What do we do about the . . . the body? It's all cold in the room but. . . ."

"If the highway's plowed maybe we can walk out and get to somebody . . . maybe tomorrow?" She looked at the door to his room. "Don't worry, we'll figure it out."

"What do you want to do with the cows?"

"Keep 'em I guess. You watch . . . be enough milk to float a battleship. Those are good cows. You'll see."

"We can't ship it."

"We can dump it for now. Just wait, you'll see."

He went down the hall with his brother and sister, put his coat on, his muscles aching, and walked out into the searing wind. "Ain't this weather somethin'?" he said.